ETHER

SEVEN STORIES

AND

A

NOVELLA

EVGENIA CITKOWITZ

FARRAR, STRAUS AND GIROUX

NEW YORK

FARRAR, STRAUS AND GIROUX
18 West 18th Street, New York 10011

Distributed in Canada by D&M Publishers, Inc.
Printed in the United States of America
First edition, 2010

Library of Congress Cataloging-in-Publication Data
Citkowitz, Evgenia, 1962–
    Ether : seven stories and a novella / Evgenia Citkowitz.— 1st ed.
    p. cm.
    ISBN 978-0-374-29887-6
    1. Identity (Psychology)—Fiction.   I. Title.

PS3603.I89 E75 2010
813'.6—dc22

                                   2009043064

Designed by Abby Kagan

www.fsgbooks.com

1   3   5   7   9   10   8   6   4   2

To my family

CONTENTS

HAPPY
LOVE

Elizabeth chose the site: the funeral was to take place under a shock of fuchsia bougainvillea at the foot of her tree; a pomegranate planted by Candayce shortly after Elizabeth was born. Seven years old and in its prime, the tree was now in full glory: slender branches with a profusion of waxy blood-veined leaves supported tumescent, ruby fruit. Candayce never got around to picking the pomegranates—in any case it might have felt a little sacrilegious. So year after year, the fruit split open and rotted on the stem, providing a feasting ground for local wildlife, mainly birds, squirrels, and worms.

Digging was harder than Candayce expected. October had been scorching. The earth beneath the tangle of weeds had cracked into scaly fissures, unyielding to the jabs of her wooden spoon. Her eyes stung, smoke from the fires still burning fifty miles away. She thought of the people whose homes had been lost, their lives, quite literally, in ashes. Yet they still talked about rebuilding. *The cost of living in beauty*, they said.

Candayce knew what they meant. It was what had brought her to California: a husband's career and a beautiful home. She was still trying to figure out what it had cost her personally. Once she had done that, she could finally ditch her shrink.

And now this.

She felt the weight of Elizabeth's sadness compounding her

own. It was unbearable to see her little face drooping with grief. Yet she was grateful to be part of it. Grateful to be given another chance. It wasn't so long ago that she could magically soothe Elizabeth's pains with a kiss.

Candayce hacked the soil, feeling shock-like spasms in her elbow and neck.

"There's a shovel hanging on the side of the shed," Elizabeth offered.

Elizabeth's presence of mind was disarming. Only minutes earlier she'd been a sobbing mass of saliva and tears. As soon as the funeral was proposed, she pulled herself together and was now behaving with all the decorum such an occasion demanded.

Candayce picked her way across the garden, past the playhouse, once her beading studio, to the shed—*so that's where it's kept*—returning with the shovel to where her daughter reverently waited.

The service was ecumenical. On a stone Elizabeth inscribed "Happy Love" and "R.I.P." above a representation of the deceased hamster in lavender gel pen. The corpse was laid on a bed of hibiscus with food and seeds for the afterlife. Then Elizabeth delivered a devastating paean: hopes for the deceased's happiness, hopes for a heavenly garden he might grow with seeds enclosed, hopes for meetings with other fallen pets. Statements of sadness and longing followed. Then it was time to say goodbye to the Corporeal Presence—Candayce had to prod her on this. Elizabeth placed the lid on the Tupperware bower and lowered Peanut into the ground.

They walked slowly back to the house. She felt the calming warmth of Elizabeth's body by her side. Until Elizabeth stepped forward and ran ahead.

It had been an overwhelming year. Candayce had only just gotten over the summer break, a two months expenses-paid holiday with Elizabeth's Anglophile grandmother in Berkshire, England, and Antibes, in the South of France. It was draining being in someone's debt that long, but Candayce had calculated the benefits for Elizabeth: an edifying European experience for her daughter was worth a little sacrifice. Staying with Elizabeth's grandmother was like living in a first-class hotel, with a domineering staff that was always watching.

On returning home, Candayce discovered the switch. The Imposter was a slug who slept day and night, a listless mound of lumpy fur. In the past, when Elizabeth was at school, Candayce would hear Peanut rustling in Elizabeth's room or a metallic twang as tooth or tail brushed against the bars of his Critter Condo. By night, Peanut was a dervish, racing across an imaginary desert in a DNA-induced panic. Round and round he went, creating a racket of beating plastic. When Peanut first came to them almost two years before, Candayce had been amazed by Elizabeth's tender care for the rodent, and her ability to fall asleep at night with him racing maniacally on his wheel.

The house was too quiet now. Thanks to all the belt-tightening Max had been talking about, there wasn't even the daily hum of the vacuum cleaner to fill the silence. The upside of her new poverty was that she liked doing her own laundry. It reminded her of bygone days when she hadn't needed an army of people to run her life. And laundry was therapeutic: the sweet, dry static of warm clothes was as satisfying as the sense of completion afterward. The downside was that cleaning for dirt was defeating. Dirt was self-perpetuating: it was everywhere and could only be kept at bay. Cleaning made her obsessive—which was why it was better someone else did it.

When Max split at the beginning of the year, telling Candayce and Elizabeth about baby Dylan, Elizabeth cried with joy at the prospect of a half-sibling while Candayce inwardly died. It wasn't so much the body blow of his treachery. She could deal with that—no one died from infidelity. It was more that the humiliation would be ongoing: that for Elizabeth's sake, she'd be forced to embrace Max's harpy attorney and his baby into an extended family group.

Candayce had known Max had wanted another child but hadn't taken in how much. The betrayal was incredible. Her friends sympathized, while secretly agreeing that they'd seen it coming. *You have to work at relationships*, they said. During all those late-night conference calls (probably phone sex), his attorney had worked at it. Candayce had not.

Less than a year before the bombshell, Max had urged Candayce to try for another baby. Candayce had turned forty and no longer had the boundless energy that had characterized her thirties. Max was freaking out about money, something to do with his deal not being renewed. Bringing another child into their stressed family unit hadn't seemed like a good idea. Yet a year and three-quarters on, Elizabeth was morphing into a young lady, Candayce could see it wouldn't be long before she was up and away. With the reasoning behind her decisions as previous as her marriage, Candayce began to wonder whether having another child would have been such a hardship, whether maybe she should have been bold and gone for it. *Maybe . . . maybe can make you crazy.* She checked herself.

"Lizzie needs a sibling. Being an only child is too much pressure," Max said.

So Candayce went out and bought her daughter Peanut.

A pet had been in the cards for a while. Elizabeth was no longer pacified by a series of canaries: Tweeties, all of them, who'd died and been replaced as necessity called. "I want a pet that will sleep in my bed," she wailed. A dog was out. Candayce knew it would be up to her to do nocturnal walking duties. She'd be damned if she would traipse through deserted Hollywood hills, the specter of the Strangler hovering over her shoulder.

Peanut was the solution. He was a fluffball of charm, with

soulful almond eyes and wavy chestnut-streaked fur. *A teddy-bear hamster, don't you know?* He was a smash hit. Candayce and Elizabeth laughed at his antics, his overstuffed pouches, and lauded his skill at navigating the tubes by smudging himself up and down. When given the chance, he could flatten under doors and squeeze himself through bars. He was the Harry Houdini of the domestic animal kingdom.

With Peanut already a bond between mother and daughter, he soon became a point of connection for others in their circle. When Uma shared Elizabeth's delight with the playful creature, it was only natural for Candayce to feel love and gratitude toward Uma, as she would anyone who happened to love Elizabeth and her furry friend.

Uma was the yoga teacher, an ethereal blond with eyes that stared in large pools of sympathy. Part two of the economy drive had been for Candayce to cut back on the private sessions with Uma, but this had proved impossible to sustain. In any case, privates at ninety dollars a pop were a mental health bargain—half of what her sometimes shrink charged. After her yoga sessions, Candayce felt her brain had been washed and balmed, her middle thoracic spine (repository of rage and anxiety) released. As a gesture to her business manager, Candayce attempted a home-practice but blanked on the sequences and cheated on the weaker side. Without Uma to cheerlead, the CNN loop showing a world with problems greater than her own was more compelling than her asanas. So Uma continued to come and generously offered to take Peanut while they were away during the summer.

First stop when they got back from Europe was to pick up Peanut from Uma's. In two months away, Elizabeth had grown an inch and matured unbelievably. Candayce was relieved to see that Elizabeth still looked forward to her reunion with Peanut with a glee that harked back to pre-K days.

ETHER

Together Candayce and Elizabeth drove downtown to Uma's studio in Silverlake. Together they stared at the mammal formerly known as Peanut. How they stared. Gone were the brown streaks that had once given him his name. This hamster's coat was streaked white and matted like an Afghan rug. Gone were the almond eyes that sometimes brought to mind her own daughter's: this one had mad, bulging orbs. His nose was bovine, not cute. Nor petite. His backside was balding and rat-like. *And he stank.* Peanut had never smelled. He'd always been a talented groomer. No way was this Peanut. More like his bad-news brother.

While Elizabeth went to the bathroom, ostensibly to wipe poop off the sad pretender's rear end, Candayce took the opportunity to whisper to Uma lightly, "What happened? Did Peanut cross over, you know, *to the Other Side?*" She made sure she used her friendliest, nonaccusing tone.

To her amazement, she saw Uma flinch.

"What do you mean? That is Peanut," Uma snapped. Her mellifluous voice, suddenly harsh and defensive.

Candayce was stunned. She'd never witnessed the dark side of Uma or seen her harden like that. Everything Uma had taught her—to give, release, and surrender—ran contrary to her behavior now.

Elizabeth returned. Although at first she'd looked shocked by the hamster's appearance, she was now cooing over it as if nothing had happened.

Candayce was reeling. She took the hamster and Elizabeth and left the studio, fast.

That night while Elizabeth was sleeping—the Imposter, flat out also (*Peanut always raced*)—Candayce paced around the cage, turning over the day's events in her head.

Was it possible that this crude substitute could be Peanut? No . . . Then why would Uma try to gaslight her? Could she have formed an unnatural attachment to Peanut and decided to keep him? That would be too risky, karma-wise, not to mention downright mean. Most likely Peanut had escaped and Uma was too guilty to cop to it.

Candayce imagined Peanut living in a crawl space at the yoga studio, gnawing his way through Uma's electrical cords. More sobering was the thought of Peanut roaming with the homeless and hungry in Echo Park.

She stopped and looked hard at the torpid creature.

Was it possible that she was imagining things and going insane?

Yes. No. Maybe.

Candayce dined out on the story, telling incredulous friends about the Switch. How she had to go along with the charade for Elizabeth's sake. How Elizabeth knew deep down but was too loving to reject him and expose Uma at the same time.

Typical of Candayce to have a psycho yoga teacher, her friends moralized.

As if the situation wasn't stressful enough, without Uma, Candayce couldn't do yoga. And she was having to avoid the cage—partly because of the smell, partly to avoid the issue with Elizabeth.

Until Elizabeth called her in.

"Mom, there's something sticking out of his cheek."

Sure enough, there was a splinter protruding from a wound in his cheek. From the bedding, they presumed.

While Elizabeth held the hamster, Candayce tried to pull out the splinter with a pair of tweezers. Nothing doing. She felt resistance as she pulled.

It must be really dug in. Urgh.

More than anything, she was surprised by the dumb creature's patience, that he didn't bite or resist.

After a flurry of telephone calls, they found Dr. Rickman, the veterinarian.

The waiting room could have been in a funeral parlor: full of wrung-out, red-eyed people waiting for word of loved ones, with no expectation that the news would be anything other than bad. Candayce had to admire their slightly ludicrous depth of feeling: impressive, when all she could feel was mild resentment of what was proving to be a three-hour ordeal.

When Dr. Rickman finally appeared, they were sitting in their designated cubicle. Candayce was startled by his creamy-faced youth. She watched him earnestly examining his patient and tried calculating his age: he looked twenty but he had to be older. *All those years of study and training.* She wondered what had made this ambitious baby know his path. Had a higher quota of mommy-love given him the advantage over all the directionless losers?

Path. Direction. Ambition. Concepts abstract and unfamiliar.

Amorphous. Mysterious. Terrifying. That was life as she knew it.

She'd known few people who were possessed with the young doctor's drive and certitude. Max was one of them. It was incredible to think that when they'd first met, her vaguely artistic, free-wheeling spirit had been something to aspire to. Something Max had respected about her. Even loved.

She felt tugging on her sleeve—Elizabeth—and heard Dr. Rickman saying, "The splinter isn't a splinter. It's a tooth."

Apparently a tooth, not sufficiently filed by gnawing, had grown through the hamster's cheek and punctured it. "You know 'rodent' comes from the Latin 'rodere'—to gnaw?" he added knowingly.

Candayce's stomach churned in horror, remembering how she'd tweezed and pulled at the hamster's cheek. No wonder she had felt resistance.

She was grateful when Dr. Rickman took him away for surgery, still nauseous when he returned half an hour later with a bloody-cheeked hamster and the tooth in a bottle for Elizabeth to keep.

The tooth looked like a tiny yellow tusk. A decayed trophy in miniature.

"Sorry," Candayce whispered to the hamster that night. "You're a brave little fella. Aren't you?" It didn't seem to matter who he was anymore. She was reminded of a movie she'd seen in her West Village days—*The Return of Martin Guerre*—but she couldn't remember whether or not Martin had turned out to be Martin. His identity can't have been that important, she concluded.

And then more horrors: the hamster started with the shitting. Candayce was already at her wit's end: no yoga, no money (Max being even more of a prick). Off they went to Dr. Rickman. Four hours and four hundred dollars later they were back at home.

Candayce had been instructed to administer two medications, two times a day. In one hand, she cupped the hamster's warm and pliant body, holding the pipette in the other. Suddenly, he opened his mouth, half-closing his eyes while he sucked the medication right up. Candayce was amazed. He looked so cute—squinting at her like a myopic uncle. And he liked the taste! The medicine was the same Barbie pink as the one she gave Elizabeth for ear infections.

He was looking at her expectantly. In fact his eyes weren't cute: they had gotten small. Candayce felt a stab. *Oh God, he's really sick. Please don't let him be really sick.*

He slept a lot. But because she didn't know him, she didn't know whether that was normal or not. His eyes stayed the same, too rheumy for Candayce's liking. Every time she saw him, she thought of his bravery that night when she'd tugged on his tooth and felt waves of guilt and affection.

This went on. The ritual, twice daily. Candayce noticed that

Elizabeth seemed to have lost interest in him. In two weeks, she had barely paid him any attention. Was it because he wasn't really her beloved Peanut? Or was she distancing herself from the inevitable—the slow death of a first love? She couldn't tell. At least she could be there for him, whoever he was. She observed the lengthening time it took him to look up at her when she called. He was winding down, like a cartoon in slo-mo.

The second Saturday after the veterinarian's, Candayce retrieved him from his cage for his afternoon meds. One thing she knew about mammals is that they're meant to be room temperature: his body had grown colder since the morning. He could barely raise his face.

He's going to die tonight. She knew it in her heart.

Unsure of how to prepare Elizabeth, she decided to say nothing. *Death is experiential. There is no preparation.*

After Elizabeth was asleep, Candayce took the Critter Condo into the stately dining room and placed it on the polished table that was never used. She sat staring into the cage, watching for his breathing, almost imperceptible now. From time to time, she took out his limp body and stroked his matted fur, uttering soothing thoughts to him. His fur was bedraggled and wet, she realized, from the tears dripping down her nose and cheeks.

Then she put him back to rest and kept vigil.

As she sat, she wondered whether his physical changes could be accounted for by illness and old age. Could sickness, combined with his dental problem, have turned Peanut's hair white and made him unable to groom—hence the smell? Had mites made him scratch away the fur around his nose, making it seem more prominent, ditto his backside?

She remembered her mother's transfiguration. The three weeks it took for her limbs to waste, her skin to turn a liverish yellow, and her mind to wash away on a sea of morphine. Afterward, the jocose Irish nurse opened the windows to set free her soul. Can-dayce looked at her mother's frozen rictus—*no soul there*—and said, "I thought the dead were meant to look peaceful."

The hamster formerly known as Peanut now rests under the shade of the pomegranate tree.

As Elizabeth said, "R dot. I dot. P dot, means rest in peace." Happy Love.

THE
BACHELOR'S
TABLE

I t could be seen through the window, standing discreetly in the corner. The moment he saw it, he knew what it was. Like a chance encounter with a deliberately forgotten love, he felt a rush of disbelief, followed by plunging disappointment and longing. He tried the door, but it was locked. The lamps outside were on, but there was no light inside. He checked his watch. Ten thirty-four a.m. He decided he would get his errands done and come back later. The place would surely be open. It was Christmas Eve after all. The busiest shopping day of the year.

He'd left the house that morning with the intention of biding his time. They'd been up since five. Jewel, walking the baby up and down, casting him reproachful glances. What more could he do? The baby was fussing and wanted only his mother. A friend's warning came to mind, that his role as dad would kick in once the child was conversational and could miss a ball without having a meltdown. Jonathan figured that might be true and hoped the best was yet to come. Cynthia was no help either, standing around waiting for drinks time. Seeing Cynthia around her grandchild supported Jewel's contention that Cynthia had been a certifiably awful mother, that a beloved Nan (no relation) had raised her. So far they'd been unable to find a Nan figure for the baby. Their last Nan had bailed.

As he walked toward the Village, the weather suddenly cleared; sunshine radiated through the cloud, illuminating the white of the clapboard houses. A series of quick calculations told him the money and stress that went into each one, a habit that came from two years' experience in the trials of second-home ownership.

The chores done. Goat's milk and espresso found. He'd also bought poinsettias and could hear their branches snapping inside their plastic bags. The cashmere scarves he'd got Jewel and Cynthia were probably redundant but they could take them back. He'd done their main presents a month ago. They'd given him a wish list from that Milanese designer on Madison Avenue. He hadn't made it to Jewel's favorite boutique with the sarongs because it was on the wrong side of town.

The wrong direction from the store.

The light was on.

He was right. He knew they'd have to open.

The old lady was sitting reading in a chair and didn't even look up when he entered. Sag Harbor had become so genteel, people didn't even worry about shoplifters. He did a circuit around the store: overpriced French provincial furniture—decorator's stuff—nothing special.

Apart from the table.

It was 1780s, made of Cuban mahogany: rich and mottled as plum pudding, smoothed by age and use. Jonathan placed his hands on the surface—for a moment he was back in his father's library—then, gripping the sides, he rotated the top around from its base.

Yes, it's what I thought.

But is it of the caliber?
On the basis of its beauty and Augustan restraint:
it was better than the other one.

His father's town house was somewhere in the eighties off Central
Park West. Jean-Pierre Edel was an art critic, known for his catalogues raisonnés and his scholarship on the Surrealist painters.
Jonathan went to his house twice, accompanying letters from his
mother asking Mr. Edel for money.

The first time they met, Jonathan was shocked to see his father
was quite old. Jean-Pierre had wiry gray hair that grew back off
his forehead as if he was facing the wind. And he was slight. In his
mind, his father had been like his first-grade sports teacher, a
muscular, thick-necked blond. He'd given him the letter without
shame or expectation. Jonathan's world was centered upon the
schoolyard: there were other boys who lived the way he did, in
cramped apartments with one parent, the other never mentioned.

Five years passed before Jonathan was sent to see Mr. Edel
again. His mother's most recent marriage had failed. Her husband,
a Great Neck Realtor, had been declared a *cunt*. Since their last
meeting, Jonathan had been able to discover little more about his
parents' relationship. All she would say was that she'd met Jean-
Pierre at an after-show party when she was still in the London
theater and they'd had what she described as a "fling."

His father smoked as he read her letter. Jonathan watched ash
fall from his cigarette and sit on his thigh like a worm. He was
trying to imagine his father on top of his mother, *flinging*, when he
caught Jean-Pierre staring at him under reptilian eyelids.

"It says here you like art?" He had a funny accent with guttural *r*'s, not completely French. "What paintings do you admire?"

His mother had tried to bring light and culture into their lives by tearing out colorful prints from magazines and taping them to the walls. On good days, they daubed together and executed garish cartoons.

"My mom's."

"I didn't know she collected." Jean-Pierre's eyes flickered, amused.

"No. She does them herself."

"Are they any good?"

Jonathan shrugged.

"What hopes do you have for your life?"

Beyond his desire for a stereo and as many albums that could fit in his stupid apartment? He conjured a serious-sounding profession.

"I hope to be a lawyer."

He saw his father's eyebrows widen, he assumed, with approval. Until Jean-Pierre said, "Good. Then you can look after your mother."

Jonathan was rebuffed and bewildered. Then repulsed. If he wasn't being mocked, could his father really mean that he, Jonathan, would have to look after his mother? The idea was obscene. Filial duty only extended so far.

His father took Jonathan around the house, showing him rooms filled with beautiful things: sculpture, textiles, more paintings than he had ever seen in his life (semi-clad ladies fleeing ghastly fates and haunting ones of half-faced girls with pointy noses).

They finished in front of the table.

His father said it was rare, made for a young man not unlike Jonathan: a gentleman with requirements, limited space, and, perhaps, means. It was a bachelor's table: writing, games, dining table, all in one. Jean rotated the top on its base and unfolded the wooden leaves, and they ingeniously butterflied out into a card table. He turned over the felt inlay and there was leather on the other side for writing. Then he swiveled the top back, eased out more panels. It expanded again into a dining table. Seeing Jonathan's delight, Jean-Pierre smiled. "I have a special affection for this piece . . ." His fingers massaged the deep, enduring surface. *"C'est un objet qui m'est cher."* He looked like a crocodile, with his eyes barely open and his unbelievably large bite.

Two years later his mother came to school. Jonathan knew what she was going to say before she said it. Jean-Pierre Edel was dead.

The house and collection were owned by an obscure French foundation. Jonathan was left nothing. No Picasso drawings. No table.

Only the memory of a smile.

"How much is this?"

He was looking at the coded label. He disliked this evasive practice, presumably designed to give the seller license to hike prices at whim.

The old lady fumbled in a ledger. There was no computer, part of the shop's faux old-world charm.

"Let me see . . . the desk. That is . . ." Jonathan watched her leafing through the pages. "Three thousand three hundred dollars."

Thirty-three hundred? It's worth ten times that!

Jonathan remained impassive. "Is that your best price?"

Her wrinkled brow folded some more. "I suppose I could give you the trade price of ten percent. That would make it . . ."

He was crouching underneath, admiring the seamless cabinetry. He looked up. "Can't you do any better? A Christmas Eve special?"

He saw that flustered her.

"Oh, I don't know. I'd have to call the owner . . ."

"No, don't bother," he quickly retracted. "Do you take credit cards?"

"A credit card will do fine."

He raced to the house for the Range Rover. *Finally, good for something.* They'd never used it for anything more rugged than trips to that inflationary grocer, Cabbages and Kings.

The table was heavier than it looked. Myrtle—so the old lady was called—hovered by, concerned he might do himself an injury. "Why don't you let me call our people? They could most likely deliver on the twenty-seventh."

"I'll be gone . . . by then." He was winded, humping it in. It was true. He had to be back on the West Coast for a meeting (unofficial: with a client's ex-partner's lawyer). He'd ship before he left. Wouldn't take any chances waiting. It was a steal.

Christmas Eve's dinner was traditionally a simple meal: cold lobster, fresh mayonnaise, and salad. Jonathan was in high spirits and bantered with Cynthia. He even risked opening a dessert wine. He knew in doing so he was flirting with disaster; experience had taught him the handling of an alcoholic parent. Jewel, with her own knowledge to call upon, was watching him, hawkeyed and suspicious.

She hadn't been impressed when he'd showed her the table.

"Is it from a ship?" she'd asked.

Although it wasn't an unreasonable surmise, he was sure she was being deliberately obtuse. "Why would you think that?"

"Oh, I don't know. Because it's kind of pokey."

"It's meant to be compact."

He knew she wouldn't like it. It wouldn't fit into her scheme of pale decorator fabrics and minimal craftsman furniture. He deferred to her regarding house décor: not because he didn't care, but because she out-cared him on the subject.

"Where are we going to put it?" was her next, inevitable, question.

They were finishing supper when Jewel saw white flakes wafting outside the window.

"Look," she cried, lifting Tommy up. "Look Tommy, it's snowing."

Cynthia jolted up, knocking over her glass with its golden liquid. "Shit," she said, dabbing her skirt with the tablecloth.

Tommy was delirious, pointing a sausage-like finger, panting, "Uh. Uh. Uh." His excitement was infectious.

"Hey, why don't I take him out?" Jonathan volunteered, full of bonhomie. Jewel approved, if only to break up the drinking party. She disappeared with Tommy and came back half an hour later with him bundled up, all down padding, practically no child.

Just in time. Cynthia was starting on him. "What bullshit imperative takes you away tomorrow? A motion to postpone December twenty-sixth?"

Jonathan carried Tommy outside, glad to escape the overheated interior and Cynthia's growlings. He stood on the porch and inhaled the sharp air, gazing out at the speckled night. Opposite, the dark leaves of a bay tree were powdered like a confection, as picturesque as could be.

Snow still held a magic for him. As a child, he'd loved it for the way it transformed the city, wrapping the careworn streets in its polar bear blanket. Only when it snowed did he experience an in-

ETHER

stant joy that didn't cost his mother anything. When two years
before he'd decided to take over the house from Cynthia—in reality, the heavily mortgaged property from the bank—he'd imagined Christmases not unlike this, although in his version, Cynthia
hadn't been quite so present, or quite so drunk.

Jonathan decided to walk on: to take Tommy to see the old
Whaler's Church. He chose the back route. It was more atmo-
spheric that way: the streets were quieter and there was less ambient light from the Village.

They went along the road, passing a cottage, all lit up and
decorated with garlands.

Everyone's home by now.

All was still. The snow was starting to settle on the ground.

It was beautiful.

Tommy threw his head back, sticking out a ruddy tongue
to catch the flakes. Jonathan grabbed his shoulders to stop him
falling.

"Ah bah, eeeh . . ."

Tommy's happy abandon was wonderful. It made Jonathan
surge with pride.

This is what it's about.

He felt an enveloping calm.

He continued on. His feet making prints, rhythmically crunch-
ing in the snow.

Left. Right. Left. Right.

Left. Right. Left . . .

A dim light wavered behind.

Jonathan looked back and saw a small car creeping slowly
along the road. Visibility was poor with the thickening snowfall.

He moved out of the road onto the narrow sidewalk.

"You know Santa's coming tonight. What do you think about
that?"

24

Tommy frowned. When he was serious, he pulled his face back into his neck and his chin disappeared into folds of creases.

"You think I'm kidding? You think I'd do that to you?"

Tommy looked perplexed. Then he smiled, radiantly baring peg teeth.

His breath was warm. It smelled of oatmeal and milk.

The light wavered again.

Jonathan glanced back.

The car was getting nearer. It was moving faster than he'd realized.

It was almost parallel now, slowing to a halt. The window rolled down and a face shrouded in a woolen scarf peered out. It took a moment for Jonathan to register it was Myrtle. Myrtle from the antique store. Her eyes looked small and startled. Weirdly, they seemed to be shining.

"Dear God. It's you!" she whispered.

"Hello," Jonathan said, surprised by her surprise.

"Oh Lord. It's really you."

Jonathan stared back. Had he missed something?

"Yep. Jonathan Edel. We met in the store."

At the mention of the store, her face seemed to sag. He realized that her eyes were shining from tears, not glee.

"Are you all right?" He had to ask.

"Noo." Her voice quavered. "Can't say that I am. I don't know how to tell you." She looked so afraid, she was starting to scare him.

"Myrtle. Tell me what?"

Then she told him.

She'd made a mistake. She'd misquoted the price on the desk. She'd missed a zero. The bachelor's table was thirty-three thousand dollars. Not thirty-three hundred. Carl, the owner, was understandably upset.

Jonathan's heart pounded and his mind raced. *So? That's how Carl gets his stock, makes a killing—by taking advantage of people's ignorance and need.*

It's still my desk.

But Myrtle was sobbing now. "I never take this road home. I don't know why I took this road. You see I was praying I'd find you. And now I have—it's a miracle."

Jonathan's back ached. Tommy's weight seemed to have doubled since meeting Myrtle. Her crying was grating. "Calm down. Please, stop crying. Give me your phone number and I'll call you tomorrow."

As instructed, she stopped crying. She looked dazed as she took a pen from a vinyl purse, writing down her telephone number on a scrap of paper. She didn't ask for his. Jonathan wondered if she was considering the possibility he wouldn't call. Passing the paper through the window, she looked up at him, her face open and full of hope. Jonathan found himself saying, "Don't worry, Myrtle. We'll work this out. Whatever happens, for God's sake, don't let this spoil your Christmas."

"Bless you, Jim. Happy Christmas."

"Jonathan. The name's Jonathan," he peevishly corrected.

Jonathan stormed back to the house with Tommy. Of all the luck, running into Myrtle. Whatever had possessed him to take the back roads?

He handed Tommy back to Jewel. Even though they'd been away less than fifteen minutes, she was happy to see him, and cooed over his cheeks that were like apples from the cold.

He didn't sleep.

What to do about the desk?

Nothing.

He would do nothing.

He didn't have to do anything. Until the morning.

He called after Christmas lunch, which dragged on with interminable amounts of food. Tommy was cranky. He'd caught a cold in the snow.

Myrtle answered after two rings.

"Hello Jim. I knew you'd call."

Jonathan was irritated. Why should she presume anything about him? *Dotty old bat.*

She told him that the store belonged to Carl Hass, that she'd only helped out occasionally as a favor. He was in Paris and anxious to speak to him.

I bet he is.

"Give me his phone number. I'll call him now." *Paris. New York. A rich man's axis.*

Carl took a while to answer the telephone. He had an educated German accent. He sounded affable. *But then he would . . .*

"We haff a problem. My dear Myrtle has made a mistake."

He said "dear." He's playing nice guy.

"You do realize the desk is worth far more," Carl said.

Well, I'll play dumb. "Oh, I wouldn't know anything about that. I just happened to like the thing," Jonathan answered.

Carl paused.

He thinks he's dealing with a moron now.

"Obviously you have the desk. It's yours. I want you to know, Myrtle won't be punished."

Jesus! A veiled threat!

"I won't be docking her pay for the rest of her young life," he added, humorously.

Oh . . . ha, ha . . .

"You know the true value of the desk is more like thirty-eight thousand dollars? It is from the 1780s, a very particular example of . . ."

Yeah, yeah. "I had no idea." Jonathan feigned surprise. "That seems rather expensive."

"I agree . . . that is a lot of money. How about I find you another desk? I have another, more beautiful one that I think you'll like as much."

No way. Jonathan chuckled inwardly. He was beginning to enjoy himself. "I don't know why, but I've become kind of attached to this one."

"Okay. How about I give you a deal? I'll let you have it for twenty-eight thousand dollars. Ten thousand less than it is worth. It was already underpriced because I was having a little problem with my cash flow. If you get it for twenty-eight, you are still making a very good deal."

He was trying to fuck him. It was inevitable.

"I don't know . . ." Jonathan paused. He could hear Carl waiting on the other end of the line. "I don't know . . . what it is about this desk. I still kind of like it." Carl would feel that like a hit. "I'll tell you what, Carl. Let me sleep on it. I never make a big decision without sleeping on it."

He heard Carl take a sharp breath, then say in his most congenial voice, "Sleep on it. Why not? Whatever is good for you. Enjoy your Christmas."

To tell Jewel or not to tell Jewel?

He told her and immediately regretted it.

"It's simple. You take it back or pay the difference." She was on all fours, busying herself with Tommy's puzzle. "You've spent enough time on it. You were on the phone for an hour in the middle of lunch."

"I wasn't talking for an hour."

She laughed, scornfully. "Why do you do this to yourself? It's all a colossal distraction."

"From what?" He knew what she was getting at but needed to hear her say it.

"It's pitiful that you have to ask." She swept Tommy up and left the room.

He hadn't been on the phone for an hour. He'd been ruminating over his conversation with Carl for an hour.

He'd have to sleep on it.

First there was present opening to get through. He liked giving gifts but not receiving them. It always led to disappointment: his own, because he never wanted anything, and the giver's, because his gratitude was never enough. This year Tommy took the pressure off them, in a frenzy of flapping tissue and shredding paper. Jewel was subdued and Jonathan made an extra effort to enthuse over the leather computer case she gave him. Not surprisingly, she and Cynthia liked their Prada bags and made noises about their scarves.

He slept on it. Or tried to. It was the worst night.

He was back on the West Coast, in their house in the Palisades. The place where he lived when he wasn't enabling a mother-in-law who failed to appreciate that if it weren't for him, she would be bellowing indigent on the street.

But the house wasn't the same.

Their sleek living room was cluttered with furniture, junky belongings of the "collectible" kind. The windows were so dirty, you couldn't see the ocean. He was arguing with Jewel. She was attacking him for sabotaging Christmas with his corrupt dealings. He was dastardly, and a failure—even Tommy agreed.

Why didn't you say "Picasso"?

He wasn't sure if Tommy had said it, or whether he'd said it himself. It didn't matter, he'd had most of his adult life to ponder Edel's question, and wonder whether he'd uttered any name other than his mother's—the greatest painter of the twentieth century might have worked—things would have turned out differently.

Why do you do this to yourself? Jewel mocked, a familiar refrain. He felt an intense hostility toward her. She had made herself his opponent, now she'd have to suffer the consequences—if he could come up with a plan. But every time he looked, the apartment was more and more cluttered, the furniture seemed to have multiplied. It was all so incredibly distracting. He had to get rid of Jewel *and* the furniture.

If only he could concentrate . . .

Suddenly, Tommy was crying inconsolably and Jewel was walking him up and down, saying, "Those are pain cries." But Tommy wouldn't stop. Soon, Jonathan was crying as well. In an effort to conceal his distress, Jonathan was swallowing his sobs, but they were going down the wrong way, making him choke. He couldn't catch his breath . . . He was suffocating . . .

He woke with a startle.

The clock said 5:10 a.m.

The relief was extraordinary.

He saw Jewel sleeping beside him, flat out, obviously exhausted. Her face had red creases from the pillows. A strand of hair had curled into her mouth. He pushed away the hair with his finger. She looked benign, not the harridan of his dream.

He was relieved that he felt no resentment toward her.

The opposite of resentment is what?

Something good.

Her only shortcoming was that she was married to him.

30

He'd get up. Wouldn't risk going back to sleep. Maybe even try to do some work, if his head would allow.

He tiptoed past Tommy's room. He could hear him chuntering happily in his crib. He'd leave him—go in only if he cried.

He felt strange. What was it? Dull from last night's alcohol and tired, yes. But he didn't feel bad.

He knew what to do.

The table was standing against the reception room wall where he'd left it. But it looked different. Somehow altered.

Jonathan squinted, kneeling down beside it. He ran his hand across the top.

Yes. It was slight, but it was there.

For a moment he wanted to blame someone: Jewel, Cynthia— even Tommy if he could. But there was no one to fault but himself.

He heard laughing inside his head before it came tumbling out. He was laughing because he'd left the table too close to the radiator and it had warped overnight. The wooden panels no longer sat flush, but undulated gently to a low truncated peak. He was laughing, because he didn't care that the table had been compromised: it was ruined before, the moment his father had shown him his rotten spoils. *Ça ne me sera jamais cher.* He was laughing because even before discovering the damage, he'd decided to take it back—take it back was what he'd do. Myrtle would tear up and thank that Christmas God of hers and say, "Bless you, Jim." Carl would have the bachelor's table restored and sell it to a customer who couldn't tell or didn't care it had been fixed.

Tommy was crying now. Jonathan padded up the stairs.

He'd let Jewel sleep in.

That would make her happy.

THE
CLEARANCE

The traffic wasn't going anywhere. The Harrods sale had just started and it had taken George twenty minutes to drive twenty inches. The fan was useless: blowing warm air, making the sweat on his forehead dry and prickle. George regretted his choice of a flannel shirt he'd chosen for its bold checks and smart country appearance. Now, with the fabric sticking clammy to his chest, he had all the time to wonder if flannel, the shirt, was named after flannel, the washcloth, for its moisture-loving properties.

When George had woken up that morning, there'd been nothing about the elements to suggest a nice day in the offing. It had been drizzling when he eased himself from under a layer of sleeping bags in such a way as to minimize aggravation to the knee that wouldn't bend. It had been raining when he'd got two telephone calls. The first was from Murray at the hospital with his wife (mysterious female bleeding), saying it was in God's hands when he'd next be able to work. The second was from Emma, reminding him to pick up Stephanie on Friday, something he hadn't forgotten but had put on the "back shelf," a place in his brain where he put all difficult tasks. It had been full-on pouring up until only a half an hour ago, when a near-miraculous parting of the cloud revealed a punishing sun that was now grilling the side of his cheek.

George nudged the van forward, braking suddenly to allow two young women to cross the road. He watched them go with a fascination that bordered on disbelief. They were different from the females he knew: they were both careless and groomed, unburdened by kids and mortgages, and ex-husbands with spreading waistlines. They brushed past into a shop selling suede coats in the middle of August, without so much as a glance at him for his small act of gallantry. It gave him little satisfaction that on the sides of their shopping bags, they'd taken with them streaks of Kentish grime from the front of his old Vauxhall van.

He was finally in Belville Place, two hours late. He cruised slowly, ignoring the bloody-minded honks of the cabbies behind. An exotic-looking woman was idling on the pavement with a Pekinese dog, waiting for it to *go*. She seemed to be all buns: two roundels on her cheeks and one on her head.

"Can't for the life of me find number four," he called to her through the window.

"Here. Here," she emitted like a squeaky toy, waving him into a disabled parking bay, in front of a double-fronted house that he'd wrongly assumed was a hotel. She pipped again that he could park there, that the traffic wardens around were "nice" and "feel sorry for the family," a possibility George thought doubtful.

"Miss Regina keep an eye out for you," she added, nodding toward the house.

George followed her glance and saw a woman standing in the swagged proscenium of the window. She was watching and waiting, like a diva anticipating her cue.

George weighed up the possibility of a clamping, that venal hostage-taking of the wheel, against the thought of putting his back out, carrying stuff miles down the road. As he was seriously late, he decided to take his chances, park, and get on.

He pressed the bell and waited on the doorstep. He was admiring the hefty ball-and-claw knocker, the panel marked "visitors" and "tradesmen" (no doubt about which one to ring), when he caught sight of himself in the polish of the fittings. Even in the burnish, his unhealthy sheen and slackening features were unmistakable. A pang of regret, and he was back, replaying the morning's conversation with Emma, which hadn't gone well. When he'd told her that he couldn't pick up Stephanie on Friday—"I'm working all day in London, and getting out will be a bloody nightmare"—she'd gone silent and he assumed that she was counting—a "coping" technique she'd learned at one of her groups. So while George waited for her to finish, he tried her counting trick. He'd got to seven before realizing she'd already hung up.

Emma's reaction to his change of plans was typical of the new Emma. When she wasn't *coping*, she was showing *zero tolerance*—buzz words that sounded suspiciously like foreign imports. Emma's cool awareness had another effect on George. It made the old days, the old-fashioned way of his mum and dad, of rowing for two days and making up for one, seem affectionate and quaintly passionate.

Emma's behavior seemed all the more unreasonable given that Stephanie was sure to be glad of the reprieve—he imagined his daughter jumping for joy when she heard. George knew that their visits had to be as testing for her as they were for him. Why else would she slouch around the flat, mute, lift up objects then put them down, and wipe her fingers afterward? (As a rule he kept the goods in the barn: they soon found their way up to the flat.) Then she'd park herself in front of the television and play video games that involved *horrendous* driving and the elimination of anyone who tried to stop her. George was surprised that Emma permitted Steph such violent content, at the same time he was grateful for the relief it afforded: relief to go in the kitchen and eat whatever he wanted, without provoking looks of disgust from his super-

cilious daughter. One of the more disarming changes he'd witnessed in Stephanie recently was a pickiness about what she ate.
Time was that she'd eat anything on offer: outings to the chippy
and conversations about the differing merits of the "Reel Deal"
versus the "Happy Meal" were what tided them through the weekend. Ever since she'd started wearing tops that showed her midriff,
all she'd eat were greens with no dressing, but she showed no
interest in accompanying him to get them at the salad bar at
Safeway.

George comforted himself, looking up and down the mansion's
handsome exterior. Gavin Bell's assistant hadn't been exaggerating
when he'd said the job was going to be "significant." First there
was the house—enormous by anyone's standards—that had defied
the fate of each of its neighbors of being divided and subdivided
into dental clinics and soft-carpeted consulting rooms. Then there
was the family, the Bratbys, whom George had looked up on the
Internet the night before. A quick glance at search results pegged
the first Lord Bratby as the illustrious one. Born Stanley Munster
in Connisbrough, South Yorkshire, he was a man of vigor and industry. It was in his towering iron furnaces, later steel mills, that
the family's fortune had been forged. He was also a talented silver-
smith as well as businessman. He'd found favor with the young
Princess Victoria through gifts of silverware he'd crafted for the
table of the royal doll's house. A specialized link praised the *superb*
quality of the service. It said that if you were to take a magnifying
glass to any platter, goblet, or feather-patterned knife, no bigger
than half your fingernail, you would have seen the royal crest
etched *perfectly* into the surface. A gift of one table setting per an-
num for twelve years to his royal friend had been enough to ensure

the ambitious Stanley Munster lasting favor and a peerage by the age of thirty.

Reading about the subsequent deaths in the Bratby male line: war, plane crash, war again, and an extremely dodgy accident, made it seem all the more remarkable to George that the Dowager Lady Bratby had died only a few months back, while she was sleeping in her own bed.

The woman from the window—*Miss Regina*—opened the door.

"George Barrow. Clearance Company," he said, trying to project cheer, at a time when his credibility was about to be flushed down the toilet. It was a disaster because not only had Murray let him down, but his other regulars, brothers Joe and Jim, had told him just the day before that they were setting up shop on their own, thanks very much. Short of picking up someone off the street, it was hard for him to find replacements at short notice. Without their hulking manpower, George was well and truly stuffed.

"Your appointment was at twelve noon," Regina said in disappointed tones, reminding him of every teacher he'd ever had. By virtue of her height, she was looking down on him.

"Sorry. The traffic was murder."

George had to force himself to look up at her, to meet her imperious gaze. She had no eyebrows, only penciled arcs. Her impatient squint told him that any further explanation would not only be pointless, but irritating.

Now she was looking behind for his nonexistent team.

"I'm just going to do a walkabout today, make an assessment. Maybe start if I can," he bluffed.

Regina looked unconvinced, knowing that hadn't been the plan at all. But now her attention was taken by the sight of his van, a filthy monolith next to a sleek bullet of a Porsche.

"Is that your vehicle?" she asked.

Before he'd had a chance to answer, she'd reached into the secretaire and taken out a disabled parking permit.

"Make sure you return it when you're done," she said, passing it to him, making George think she wasn't such a dragon lady after all.

The entrance was set with murals in amber tones, depicting pastoral scenes. It took a second glance for George to register that they were Spanish and early, and made out of embossed leather. Mottled Venetian glass, fashionable with decorators of a certain period, continued where bucolic scenes left off. The vestibule then opened into a large hall, with a staircase that went up and up, and was lined with ancestral prints.

Regina led George like a fifties model: shoulders back, hips forward, swishing a maroon pleated skirt as her curiously large feet pointed the way forward. George followed with a swaying gambol-cum-fast-walk he'd developed to avoid putting too much weight on his right side. He would have happily lingered to take in a portrait of a flushed youth, some lovely porcelain, a spectacular chandelier, and all the plush furnishings he could wish for, tagged and ready for pickup by Gavin's crew, but she was moving too briskly. He glimpsed a belter of a long case clock (he'd always respected clocks; they embodied a stately certitude lacking in his own life), but a sharp backward glance from the Eyebrows told him not to be so nosy and to keep his eyes to himself. They passed through a door and were on the back stairs, bare and austere after the opulent front. The staircase narrowed as they descended. The scratched wooden steps gave way to weathered York stone, smooth from a century of feet scurrying attendance on the troubled Bratby family. The smell of must and damp flagstones, recently washed with just a hint of bleach, mingled with the sweet odors of roast chicken and two veg. He felt his shoulders loosen and his soggy chest lift and expand. Even though he'd never been there before, he had a sense of return. Like a badger to his set, basements were his habitat. A place where he belonged.

George had come to his line of trade after a two-year stint working at his father-in-law's newsagent's, something he hadn't enjoyed. He'd found it claustrophobic dealing with customers all day: the pensioners who'd come in for the newspaper and wouldn't leave, spending the day bending his ear, making him reach for another Twix. Then there were the lippy light-fingered kids who'd arrive like a plague, reminding him of school, where he'd been miserable because chubby boys were expected to be jokers or play silly buggers, and he'd lacked the personality to do either. George would sit paralyzed behind the counter, stricken all over again, as he watched the boys cavort around in the aisles, stuffing Cadbury's down their shorts. George turned a blind eye rather than risk confrontation, but he was left in a constant state of panic, knowing the books wouldn't add up come stocktaking time. When Emma's dad finally installed a security camera, George knew it was time to move on. He scoured the employment pages of the local newspapers and answered an ad: WANTED—MAN WITH A VAN. A week later, after the quick purchase of an eighties Vauxhall, George was working for Monty Castle, who did house clearances.

We go in after the family have squabbled over the furniture and the antique dealers—bloody crooks—have cherry-picked the best bits and everyone is too shagged to care about the rest.

It was George's job to get rid of the stuff that no one wanted, usually after a death, divorce, or bankruptcy, enabling his clients to start a gathering and accumulation of their own, so that the process could be repeated again by their children or executors in another sixty years.

George quickly learned that stuff no one wanted had a surprising value, once you'd sorted what was unsalable. Stained mattresses and mildewed books were worth zero on the retail scale; likewise newspapers and magazines dated after 1945 were for the dumpster. Curtains with sun or water damage weren't worth bothering with, and Monty had never had luck with clothes, unless from the sixties or earlier—they were taken straight to the charity shop. The money was in the remaining items: ceramics, paperbacks, utensils, side tables that just needed a lick of paint, tarnished metalware that cleaned up nicely, even old postcards and photographs, if they were sold to the right collector. Sometimes, in the bigger jobs, a large object—a plain Victorian nursery cupboard worth a few hundred quid—would be left because no one wanted the hassle of moving and consigning it to a lesser showroom, so it would be left for the clearance people, a bone for the dog.

Meeting Monty was more than fortuitous, because at Castle Clearances George discovered something he could do. His taciturn nature was suited to handling and sorting, and he had the nose and instinct for the hunt: all he needed was a whiff of possibility and he'd be off in dogged pursuit, until something worth finding would be found and a monetary killing would be made. But his interest wasn't only financial. George had a deeper connection with his work. There was an absorbing mystery attached to an object: stripped of context, with its history forgotten, all that was left was the thing itself, it became pure again—pure as when it had first been made. And yet, very occasionally, with certain things, George felt something more: the residue of the previous owner, imprinted in the gnarled fabric of a child's toy or the whorls of a tortoiseshell hair ornament. When that happened,

George was warmed by the knowledge that probably he alone recognized the special significance of the item. These quiet moments
gave George confidence and pride. They were, for him, an occupa-
tional privilege. Even as a child George had been drawn to the
cozy clutter of a local junk shop. On his way home from school, he
and his sister, Katy, would linger outside the store, Katy to smoke
by the racks and catcall to the boys as they went past, George to
view the wonders of a basket marked sixpence: a glass decanter
stopper, a frayed leather purse, a domino, and a bead that looked
like a sapphire. The owner had taken a liking to George. He never
liked Katy—didn't trust her darting eyes and cadging ways. He let
George polish fenders in return for a free dip at the basket. George
chose the sapphire first, followed by the purse. His innate savvy
told him not to choose the domino.

It was directly because of Monty Castle that George was doing the
Bratby residence today. Just as Joe and Jim—*navvy bastards*—
would go on to exploit contacts they'd made working for George,
it was through Monty that George had met Gavin Bell. They'd
met on a job in Chelsea. George had gone with Monty to do a flat,
a redbrick affair that belonged to a "rich old bird" who'd "hopped"
(Monty's words). As usual, probate had been done; the relatives
had marked objects for keeping with coded stickers. The best
pieces had been designated for sale by the auction house: Castle
Clearances was to handle the rest. George and Monty had picked
their way through the usual bric-a-brac: tourist souvenirs culled
from warmer climes. They had managed to score with some decent Regency washstands. In the sitting room, they found a pile of
mawkish paintings, most probably done by the deceased because
they had been marked for the tip. ("We simply don't have the
room," the daughter sighed.) Also in the pile was an oil sketch of a

middle-aged woman with lively eyes, which George had a feeling about. So at the end of the day when Monty was out smoking, George went in search of a higher authority, which he found in the shape of Gavin Bell (in those days a lowly saleroom assistant recently down from the Courtauld, not the senior player he was later to become). Gavin had just finished the catalogue and was getting ready for his bike ride home. He was bending down, strapping a herringboned leg inside its cyclist's clip, when he saw (upside-down, as it were) George's lumbering figure coming toward him, the picture pressed to his chest. The sketch was presented to Gavin. Gavin, dizzy from standing up too quickly, cast an eye over it before agreeing that, perhaps, it deserved a little further research. When the picture was later revealed to be the "old bird" herself by Augustus John, the family was thrilled. The credit for the discovery went to Gavin, and George, whom Gavin now regarded as very honest or very stupid—it didn't matter which—earned himself Gavin's loyalty. From that point onward, George Barrow became his clearance man of choice. This minor discovery gave George the confidence to set up on his own in a barn adjacent to a petrol station off the M25. Emma was pregnant with Stephanie and pressuring him to give up his gypsy existence for "a proper job." A proper job, by her definition, was never going to happen, but starting a small business felt like a step in the right direction. Although his new enterprise lacked the regularity of a nine-to-five position, George was glad to be his own man.

Regina led George along a corridor snaked with pipes and wiring, past a mahogany box housing the old servants' bells ("Lord Bratby's Dressing Room, Lady Bratby's Bedroom"), turning right where the passage branched into two. There were three doors on either side with a barred exit to an outside stairwell at the end. She opened and closed the three doors on the left, giving him a heart-thudding preview of the scale of his task; it was massive—far bigger than he'd expected. Each room was filled with a century's detritus. Then Regina turned and opened the three doors on the right.

She was in the last of the rooms and didn't look up when they entered. Half-obscured by boxes and packing cases, she was kneeling in the corner reading a letter. Nearby, George saw a fitted cupboard hanging open. It was stacked with dusty papers—more letters judging from their size and the way they were bound. From what he could make out in the half-light—the windows at the back were filthy and the room's subterranean aspect ensured it would be perpetual dusk in there—her hair was bark-colored and had a shock of white at the front. He thought she looked about the same vintage as he, which was forty-odd. For George, forty was a great leveler. Anyone over was plodding or jogging (for the super-fit) the same path to the same destination, whereas anyone younger was dancing, recklessly, in whatever direction they fancied.

George immediately saw the containers had recently been rifled: the overflow was much cleaner than the remaining jumble of defunct electrical goods, ubiquitous beds (there must have been five), and packing cases that were layered with dust. He guessed the last time these quarters might have been inhabited was before the war.

"That's the last one," Regina said, and closed the door behind them.

Usually George and Murray had a system. They'd start outside and work inward, hauling the large items to a skip to get them out of the way. But today, there was no skip because there was no

Murray, Joe, or Jim. After showing the rooms, Regina had told him, "The Trustees expect George Barrow Clearances to have completed services by the end of the week," a sharp reminder of the hopeless reality of his situation. He sweated anxiously before quickly resolving a plan. He had to at least try to create an impression that inroads were being made, so he decided to work as long as possible and then later—he had no choice—he'd trawl the pubs and enlist anyone who had two arms and a leg to come and help the next day.

On his way back upstairs, George took a wrong turn and ended up in the kitchen. It had long pantry cupboards and an antique iron range. With the exception of a few electric appliances and the Belling stove in the corner, it was like viewing a scene from the beginning of the last century.

The Bun Lady was apparently cook as well as dog walker. She was there, stirring something on the stove.

"Just trying to find my way out—get some dustbin bags out of the van," George told her.

She reached into a drawer and pulled out bag after bag, flourishing them like a magician with scarves. "You like the house?" she said. The glint in her eyes told him she knew the answer.

"Fairly impressive, I have to say."

"Lady Bratby like a mother to me. She say 'Don't go until they gather me up.' So I stay until she die. You need more?" She proffered the box.

"If they're spare, thanks."

She handed him the whole box, extravagantly, as if rubbish was no object.

"I leave tonight and no come back. After tomorrow, they come and take everything. It no be the same." She screwed up her nose with displeasure. On hearing the words "they take everything,"

George could only wish that included the shitload of stuff in the basement.

George opted to start in the far corner room on the right. It was the most densely packed—a question of tackling the worst first. He sidled to the end, sucking in his girth to navigate the tighter spots. His intention was to start black-bagging newspapers (why did people hoard them, a known fire hazard? and beds, when they took up so much room? It was something of a nonstarter, the chance that long-departed family and friends would suddenly appear for a massive sleepover). He was scooping up his first armful of newsprint, pondering the relationship of the Bun Lady and the expired dowager, this Lady Bratby, who had been as beautiful as Louise Brooks in her youth, and formidable as Margaret Thatcher in her old age, when he heard a groan.

He stopped.

Then another.

There it is again.

He'd been so preoccupied that he'd forgotten all about the lady in the corner. It was incredible to think he must have walked straight past her! George felt blood rush to his face. Was she ill or having some sort of reverie, presumably of a private kind? Her moans were low and insistent. To his embarrassment, it was a bit sexy, like a porn star's pleasure (yes, he'd watched the dirty videos that he'd found at the back of many a cupboard).

"I knew it," she whispered to herself. "Here . . . all this time." Her words sounded like exhalations of shock and disbelief.

George caught the unhappy tremor in her voice. It cut through any fantasy that she might be giving herself a good time. As she clearly didn't know he was there, George thought it time to make himself known. He grabbed a chair with the intention of using it to scrape back and forth to make a noise, but succeeded only in destabilizing a mattress, that fell on a lamp, that knocked into a tower of boxes, one of which toppled into her corner.

He heard her give a more prosaic *oof* of surprise.

Now the cardboard wall was half down, George could see her flush with annoyance.

"You all right?" he asked, feeling like a prize chump.

"Fine," she snapped, giving the box an aggressive shove back into its place.

George reckoned the woman had to be Lady Miranda, Lady Bratby's only child. He hadn't read up on her—not that there'd been much to read, cyber-wise. He recalled that she was made out to be something of a recluse-slash-bag-lady, the kind that aroused a mixture of pity and disdain in the popular press. There had been plenty of info about her mother's colorful life, and lurid accounts of her father's death in a bizarre autoerotic mishap. He recalled there was something about Lady M.'s engagement, some twenty years before, but couldn't remember seeing anything about marriage or kids.

"This is hopeless—to be reading here," she said, and then asked him for help.

She carried one stack of letters from the cupboard, and he the remainder, cradled in his arms. They went upstairs, the labyrinthine back way. He trod carefully: he didn't want to fall and damage the correspondence: it looked brittle enough as it was. He did manage to peek down as he went: the letters were addressed in feathery hieroglyphs to Lord Bratby of Belville Place. Where the ribbons had loosened around the knots, he could see a true apricot color, budding in the gray.

By the third floor, the carpeting—a velvety wall-to-wall in dusty rose—signaled they were nearing the private areas. One more corridor, and sure enough, they were in a large room that had to be the master bedroom and must have therefore belonged to the late Lady Bratby. The walls were hand painted with birds that swooped up and down, ribbons and bows in their beaks, rising to a crested heart above a voluptuous super king. The canopy matched the pale flounces on the dressing table.

She told him to put the papers down there, on the bed. "It's the only surface that isn't being sold."

It was awkward being with her in the bedroom: too intimate and feminine to be appropriate—it was like accidentally straying into the ladies' room. So when she smoothed her hair and thanked him—tantamount to a dismissal—George was only too happy to go.

He went back down to the basement, managed fifty bags, and was halfway up the stairs, struggling with numbers fifty-one and fifty-two, when Regina appeared on the top landing. She'd changed into a long dress and had put makeup on, her eyelids painted an iridescent turquoise. She was back in dragon-lady mode. She ordered him to leave: she was locking up.

Lady Miranda must have been in the kitchen because she was suddenly at the bottom of the stairs, calling up, "He can stay as long as he wants—the night, as far as I'm concerned."

Her intercession was stunning.

Equally surprising was the way Regina ignored Lady Miranda and turned on her heels, without acknowledging her suggestion.

George's first reaction was that Regina must have taken offense at being overruled in front of a tradesman. His next thought was that there was some sort of bitch-feud going on—that much was clear from the way the ladies wouldn't even look at or speak to each other. Whatever it was, for once George wasn't blaming himself. He was already overloaded with crap. He was fed up, full up—no room for any more. Instinct told him he had nothing to lose by the situation, so in a moment of fantastic boldness he stammered, "Actually, it would be great if I could stay—if it's no trouble, that is. I've got loads to be getting on with and it would save a lot of time on the commute."

George saw Regina stop in her tracks and slowly turn. By the time he saw her face, her pencil-brows were up at her hairline. A vein, the same color as her eye shadow, had popped like a lightning bolt across her forehead, and there was another zigzagging across what looked like an Adam's apple. George thought she might explode.

Instead, Regina laughed, a deep and throaty laugh, and said incredulously, "You want to stay the night?"

George nodded meekly, his nerve quickly failing.

"All right," she said. "It's not as if we don't have enough room."

Then she strode back upstairs, leaving George, gobsmacked, to get on with his work. When he looked back to thank Lady Miranda, she had already gone, he assumed, back to the kitchen, to do whatever she was doing before—maybe eating, if she had any sense.

An hour later Regina returned and took him to the top of the house. On their way, they met the Bun Lady coming down the stairs. She was buttoned into an unseasonably thick overcoat and was carrying two small suitcases in her hands. She didn't stop. Just muttered a quick goodbye as they passed. She seemed to be in a hurry to leave.

Regina and George continued up, until they reached what must have been the old nursery floor. At both ends of the landing, he saw low wooden safety gates, and something about the wallpaper—faded cherries—made George think of children. Regina then showed him the bedroom where he could sleep. It was small. It had a single bed with a cambric bedspread, a dresser, and a sewing machine that still had a spool of pink satin thread in it. She showed him the bathroom a few doors down, and told him that she'd set the alarms at midnight and not to do any "wandering" after that. (Her eyes might have twinkled, but he couldn't be sure.) Regina told him there was food in the kitchen, that he could help himself if he liked. George was relieved to hear that. He could go long hours without eating, as long as he could make up for it later.

"Thanks very much," he said, genuinely grateful.

He worked until 11:30, then went into the kitchen and nibbled on some bread and cold chicken that had been left out on a plate. He was uncharacteristically un-hungry, probably from nerves and the strangeness of it all. Then he went upstairs and ran himself a bath, stealing a drop of Floris Ormonde from a bottle in the cabinet.

Floating in the water, George inhaled the steaming aromas. His eyes were closed: he never looked at himself if he could help it. The heat of the water was calming and helped ease the strained muscles in his back. Lying in the dark, he could almost convince himself that everything was going to be all right.

He hopped back to his room, a towel around his waist. The sheets were cold and starched and he shuddered as he slipped naked between them. Just before midnight, he turned off the lights. A minute later, he heard a robotic voice: the sound of the alarms being armed.

He smiled to himself. Regina was true to her word.

He wasn't sure how long he was asleep before she came in. He woke up and saw Lady Miranda standing at the foot of the bed.

She was in a smocked nightgown that reminded him of a shepherd he'd seen in the murals downstairs.

"Could I come in?" she asked.

You are in. "Yeah, of course," he said, quickly gathering his senses.

She moved around the side of the bed. She looked younger than he'd first estimated—maybe as much as ten years, possibly more.

"You must think I'm mad, barging in . . ."

"No, I wasn't asleep," he lied, pulling up the sheets to his neck.

"I can't sleep. It's coming back here . . . you leave a place for a reason."

George nodded. He thought he knew what she was getting at about the house. It felt abandoned. Not that it bothered him: pathos was part of who he was and what he did.

She stared at him—rather, in his direction. Her eyes looked out of focus, as if she was looking at some other thing in her eyeline, and he just happened to be in the way.

In the absence of words, George nodded again, like a bobbing dog on a dashboard. He was trying to look sincere, in an effort to distract her from an erection that was lifting the covers from his thighs.

He saw her shiver. It was hot in the day but the temperatures plummeted at night.

George felt he couldn't lie there, watching her tremble in the cold. He had to do something to comfort his insomniac visitor. There was nothing for it but to lift the covers and offer her the warmth of his own body—even if it meant exposing his baser nature.

She looked at him, impassive. She went to him: sitting first, before folding up her legs and lying down, her back to his side.

It was minutes before she spoke again.

During that time, thoughts came flickering to him: the yellowed letters, the dragon lady (*she a bloke?*), Emma's eternal rage (*justified, of course*), Katy (*she'd almost be an old lady if she were alive*), and Steph (*hope she does better in life than me and her mother*). His thoughts returned to Katy, as they nearly always did. Katy, who loved to do the undoable, say the unsayable. He'd often wondered what her life would have been like if she'd survived.

He had two portraits of her in his mind. The first was of a cleaned-up, mellow old girl, living in a cottage somewhere, doing something wholesome such as baking, gardening, or knitting. In this honeyed version, it didn't matter whether she was single or divorced because she was all right in herself: she'd got her act together and was finally taking care of business. The other Katy was a more alarming prospect, probably closer to the truth of what she would have become: a ranting, raven-haired witch. She was alone, not through any choice of her own. Her caprices had long stopped being amusing to anyone other than herself. He saw her lips, puckered from incessant smoking. They were still angry, full of trespass and regret. The lips she used to press into his when she wanted him to keep a secret. So many secrets.

These images came to him, and, mercifully, they went.

Finally, she spoke.

"It was up here, in this room, where I found him." (The words "found" and "him" were enough to clue in George.) "She made it look as if it was an accident. A *mis*take. He would have left her if he'd survived."

Apart from her articulation of "mistake," which she made sound like a sharp cutting instrument, there was little emotion in her voice.

"I knew all this time, but the letters prove it. They're written to my father by his lover of ten years. Replies to his, except the one he wrote the day he died. He promised to join her later that day—

said he was leaving this house for good. My mother found out and stopped him. The letter was never sent. Someone hid the letters who knew the truth, understood their significance—who realized they must be preserved until it was safe."

George pondered the scenario. He agreed that if you were eloping with someone, stringing yourself up for a bit of autoerotic satisfaction wouldn't naturally take precedence over getting the hell out, but then again, as George knew, the human heart and all its recesses could be an unfathomable and darkly illogical place. Hadn't the letter said something about leaving the house for good? Whether Lord Bratby's death was a suicide, accident, or murder, George understood that her accusation befitted the trauma she must have suffered all those years before. Her scars were familiar, the kind he lived with and took everywhere he went. Like hers, they were formed by loss. Hers, from loss and a terrible suspicion. His, from the loss of Katy.

George was ten when he and his sister had taken a detour home from school. It had been her idea not to go the boring pedestrian route but to clamber along the bank of the railway instead. Where the tracks met the overpass, Katy had made him wait by the signal box, while she climbed up and shimmied across the narrow sidings of the bridge. He'd had serious misgivings but done nothing to warn her. He knew how caution always had the opposite effect on her intended—he already had the sense that she was challenging him *not* to stop her. She was smiling at him and he back, when she'd leaped to her death onto the tracks below. It happened so quickly that when he heard her body hitting the ground, a deflated crunch as bones and organs compacted, George's face was still creased in a stupid grin. In all the time that had passed since her death, George's relationship to it had shifted only in that he'd stopped asking himself why he hadn't been able to prevent it: he'd come to believe there had been a certain inevitability about the event. The questions that stayed with him, that undermined him still, were the same ones he'd asked himself over thirty years before: why Katy had felt the need to hurt herself, whether puncturing her arms with nail scissors, or making welts on her thighs with a scented candle from Boots. Or her final dance on the bridge that felt so much like an act of defiance. Defiance of what? The why of it had never been answered by the explanation that she wasn't normal. That Katy wasn't like anyone else.

The cold seemed to emanate from her body.

"You're freezing," he whispered, turning toward her.

He was just about to say it but she said it first: "We don't have to do anything if you don't want"—an uncanny echo of his thoughts.

He did want. But he knew he would suppress it, as was his way.

Her hand, so cold, reached behind and found his arm, gently bringing it forward, wrapping it around her shoulder and tucking it under her breast like a comfortable blanket. He went limp—which was more than fine—it was enough to be so close to her and feel her warming in his arms. More wonderful was the sense, as he fell into a deep, contented sleep, that he could have told her anything: his fantasies or failures. But there was no need. Somehow, she already understood.

George woke up early and she'd gone. He wasn't surprised. With the first light of day, he'd had an uneasy dawning—it came slowly at first, creeping across the back of his consciousness. It was a feeling that hardened into certainty that something was not right. Something was amiss.

He was still putting on his shirt as he went down the stairs, stumbling two steps at a time. Only later did it occur to him that he might have set off the alarms if they'd been armed on the back stairs.

But he wasn't thinking about alarms.

He was thinking about the cupboard in the last room.

The cupboard was locked: the doors sealed over with layers of paint, as George suspected. He found his crowbar and forced the doors open. The wood cracked and splintered, releasing a thick, fungal dust as it gave. He coughed, his lungs rejecting the dust. When he saw what was inside, his stomach sickened.

The letters were there—covered in a layer of thick London soot, untouched since they'd been put there more than half a century before. He stared at them, while his heart that had so recently felt a fullness of possibility drained and emptied. He didn't need to go back online to check, because there on his back shelf was the obituary of Lady Miranda Munson he'd seen two nights before. It was only one line, with her birth—November 30, 1931, and her death, November 30, 1980—no mention of the cause, just a line indicating a link to more information, but he'd skipped over it in favor of the one about Princess Victoria's silver.

His head was beginning to throb, heavy with the sensations of his encounter.

She was right about the house. It wasn't good for anyone.

He dropped to his knees, the same spot where he'd first seen her kneel (his right knee, no choice but to buckle with him). He set to work on the cupboards. He ignored the papers: they were work for an archivist and weren't what he was looking for in any case. Reaching inside, his fingers explored up and under the fractured door, searching for hidden ledges on which valuables might have been secreted. Experience had taught him that people hid things: for safety (*ha!*) or as an act of control or power. He was sure he'd find something; that his hand would soon close around the cool facets of a stone, or some other rare and precious thing.

It wasn't only his head that was pounding, but his heart. It was doing a demented dance. *Boom tiddly, boom-boom.*

Bloody dust.

It was making him wheeze, but he knew he would find something if he kept going.

He'd find something, maybe to give to Stephanie.

Something worth keeping.

Even if it killed him.

SUNDAY'S
CHILD

I found a girl in the playhouse last week.
She was curled up on the loveseat, her back to the door.
She was too big to lie straight.
Her feet were crooked at an angle over the armrest.
She'd taken off her trainers, laid them neatly on the floor.
She was young. I could tell.
On the back of her head: a flaxen braid.
She had one of Ambrose's blankets pulled around her shoulders.
Orphan Heidi with a shawl.
When I first saw her, I had this crazy dialogue with myself:
oh, that doll looks like a person.
Actually, that person looks like a doll.
No, that person looks like a person.
By then I was walking backward out of the playhouse,
trying to rewind myself out of there.
To get to the place where I was before I saw her.
I told myself she could be dangerous.
She could be on crack.
She makes me scared.
She must go.

ETHER

I'd planned to do something nice with Ambrose over the break. To take him for a dip in the ocean, see what he'd make of ducks in the canyon, but the storm came in, and we ended up staying at home, watching cartoons, and stacking, because he likes to stack, and it was the only thing that distracted him from the rain. The storm really frightened him. The rain was intense: nonstop for ten days, beating at the windows, drumming on the roof, water rushing down the hill, full-on like a running faucet. His whole body went stiff and he held his head cocked to the side, ready to snap around as if something bad was going to happen. At night, he had his eyes locked on the ceiling like he thought it was going to collapse. With Ambrose, the difficulty is trying to differentiate between what's normal, and something else—something that relates to something that happened before we met.

It didn't take me long to figure out that his fear was not the healthy kind.

In the six months since I picked him up from the foster home, he's been a restless sleeper. A night hasn't passed without him padding in and getting in my bed. So now, when it's bedtime, I put him directly into my own room.

I don't know what else to do.

He seems to be doing better. He sleeps splayed over me, sucking into me like a starfish.

At least someone is sleeping.

We didn't see anyone for weeks. I didn't feel like being around friends with their opinions, when I know they think that I'm insane to have taken him on. I got sick of the sound of my own voice. The coaxing voice. The soothing voice. The keep-it-together voice. And the manipulating one. Anything to draw him out. I know he's in there somewhere.

Sure, the storms affected me. They made me realize how Southern Californian I've become. After thirty years, I've finally acclimatized. Rain is now an event. At the first signs of it, I drive very slowly and hunker down in front of the TV—nothing like watching the rest of the world going to shit from the comfort of your own home. It's a deprivation being without light, and everything feels subdued: the traffic's barely humming, even the neighborhood dogs have shut up with the yapping. When they issued a mudslide warning, I went out with my flashlight and looked at the hillside—like I'm suddenly an engineer—and convinced myself that my neighbor's extension was about to surf down and bury us in a wave of mud. Afterward, when I went in, I caught sight of myself in the mirror: black garbage bag tied round my head and shoulders—all I had in the rainwear department. My nightshirt was wet through, see-through, clinging to an ass as large and pitted as the surface of the moon. I looked at myself and thought, *Intriguing European ingénue well and truly gone. Blousy LA loon, how the heck are you?*

He's back at school now.

You'll be glad to know it was chosen in consultation with an army of therapists and counselors.

Glad because it means I listen to the advice of esteemed professionals such as yourself . . .

Seriously, the school's a perfectly good Montessori run by two perfectly good dykes.

It was good of them to have us. They could have easily said no because Ambrose needed a special school. They're working with us on the understanding that we'll reevaluate every six months.

I'd say the first six months at school were a pretty good nightmare.

For one thing, I was concerned that Ambrose was being ostracized.

When parents saw us coming, they'd scatter, or become *very involved buckling the backpack*. Anything to avoid talking to us.

Because, let's face it, he's a little weird. He's black and they can't figure out what he's doing with a fat white woman and they're terrified I might ask for a playdate.

A playdate.

I'd see other mothers at school pulling out agendas, setting them up. I came to *loathe* the expression *playdate*. Instead of saying, "Why don't you bring child-in-question over to play?" they said, "Let's set up a playdate." You've got to admit, it's a terrible combination, "play" and "date." Where's the fun in "date"? Where's the spontaneity and innocence?

My point is that no one seemed to care that Ambrose had no one to schedule with.

No one except me, and Reese.

Thank God for Reese.

When she left her message, "Reese Poley here, Cameron's mother. Hope you survived the rain," pleasant chuckle. "We wondered if Ambrose would be available for a playdate before school starts up," I could have wept, or burst into song:

Hallelujah. Hallelujah. A playdate at last.

When that wore off, I wondered, *Why Ambrose?* Then I remembered seeing Reese outside the school gates, distributing flyers for a children's hospital. And then I remembered hearing that Cameron had heart problems when he was a baby. I put the two together. She's seen me struggling at drop-off time. Ambrose, being prized off my legs by the teacher's assistant. She's noticed that Ambrose is the only one who doesn't cluster with the others at the Lego table, who isn't coloring nicely at pickup time. He's the one sitting silently in the corner, who never answers Miss Adams's *Good mornings* or *Goodbyes*.

She felt sorry for us.

You'd have to.

It was a *pity-date*.

I didn't care. We'd take what we could get.

They didn't find any physical brain damage, but there's damage that doesn't show up on scans. The kind I see every day. We know that his mother's prenatal diet of crack cocaine didn't exactly boost his IQ, and there's three and a half years of trauma and neglect to factor in. We have a pretty good idea why he's not talking.

The term they're using is *selective mutism*—an adaptive response to stressful circumstances. It's the only diagnosis that doesn't actually faze me.

It makes total sense.

Hey, I don't feel like talking when I don't get my *latte* . . .

I'm not in a relationship.

I suppose my only relationship of significance was with Jeremy. We were together eighteen years. I moved in with him as soon as I arrived in California. He gave me my first role, which got me the series that set my career on its path to mediocrity. He lived in a huge white stucco house, with blue and gold-leaf tiles and a minaret. He had this ugly great African grey parrot, Oscar, who used to terrorize me. Whenever I came near, he'd fly at me. Would have pecked out my eyes if he hadn't been manacled to his perch.

Some hilarious person had taught Oscar to say *Bugger off bitch*.

He was always telling me to *Bugger off bitch*. He never said that to anyone else.

Cute, huh?

Well I can be cute, too.

I'd whisper back, "Guess what gray bird is going in the *tangine* tonight? *Notapigeon*."

When Jeremy wasn't working, he loved to entertain. The house was always full of interesting people: writers and artists; part commune, part salon. I'd like to think I amused him a little. I was outrageous in those days, always clowning around, doing imitations, whatever it took to make people laugh.

We were lovers at the beginning, but the transition into a sexless partnership was fairly seamless.

I can't remember . . .

Was it after about six or seven years?

By the time I was thirty?

Then he got sick, a long and horrible decline. At the end, I kept a vigil—with about fifty of his closest friends. We got drunk on whiskey we'd sneaked into the hospice. We were all so busy talking—loud and emotional—no one heard the monitor going off. It was only when the nurse came in we realized that Jeremy had died in front of us and we hadn't noticed. I felt terrible about that. Jeremy would have hated the carelessness. He was always very meticulous—and something of a diva. All directors are.

I miss him.

He was good to me.

He gave good advice.

When you reach my age, you won't need a lover. You'll need real estate. Be smart. Don't fritter your money away. Put it into a house or an apartment. You'll be sorry if you don't.

That's what I did. When I got my first paycheck, I bought my house. The neighborhood was borderline then: a mixture of hippie types like me, and low-income families. It's changed beyond recognition. It's still changing: every single house on my street has scaffolding on it.

I'm okay financially. I still get residuals. Jeremy left me some money.

Roger got the house.

Roger was his boyfriend. Jeremy was incapable of being monogamous.

Roger got the house because Jeremy knew I could take care of myself—I can always play somebody's mother in a sitcom, or do voice-overs.

Roger needed the house with all his medical bills.

Yes, I've been tested.

Yes, I'm all right.

Then there was no one for a while. Then there was Howard. That lasted three years. Howard was Jeremy-lite. I say that because they had the similar way of looking at things, very aesthetic and social, but he didn't have . . . he wasn't Jeremy. By the time I met Howard, I was tired of being bossed around and too old to care whether the candlesticks matched the tablecloth. I was with him another five years, up until a few years ago.

We split up because Howard was opposed to adoption. That doesn't mean that we wouldn't have broken up. The adoption issue just speeded things along.

He said he didn't want to adopt because he'd had a horrible childhood. His parents were abusive. He'd make lame excuses like *I do not want to go back there.*

As if adopting a child would take him *back there.* As if that's the issue. As if going back is ever an option. How great would it be if it were? We'd all be going *back*—lines around the block— changing everything we ever did.

What was I like when I was with Jeremy?

Good question.

Maybe this will give you some idea.

A journalist once asked Jeremy about me. He said something like *She's a consummate actress. When she's not in character, it's hard to know who she really is.*

I was devastated when I read that: shattered that he saw me that way. As far as Jeremy was concerned, he was paying a compliment, high praise *for an actress.* Really he was saying that I had no personality. That there was no there, there.

I never told him how much that hurt.

Didn't want a fight.

Didn't think it would make any difference.

When I was making the decision to adopt, I asked myself all the big questions:

I might have twenty more years, what could I hope from them?

Can I go through with the adoption?

Should I go through with the adoption?

Jeremy's words kept coming back to me.

I realized what he'd said about me was true. When I look back, I see someone so pale and shapeless. I'm barely there.

If Jeremy could see me now, he wouldn't recognize me.

Why?

I'm showing all my colors. Light through dark.

I'm blazing in Technicolor now.

Oh there, I knew I could make you smile.

The actual adoption process wasn't difficult at all. I got Ambrose online.

It's true. I'm not being disrespectful or facetious.

Let me explain something. There's a whole fuckin' hierarchy when it comes to adoption. If you're not young, married, and wealthy, you can forget about adopting a white baby. You're not even allowed near the list to adopt a white baby. You are, however, considered good enough for another group of children, who are, I hate to say it, undesirables. Undesirable, because they're older; they're black and Hispanic; they've been in and out of foster homes and institutions; they have health and developmental issues and come practically certified with emotional problems. Unlike the white babies, for which there's a waiting list as long as your arm, there's plenty of the others available to the un-rich, unmarried, and un-young.

So the process of getting Ambrose was relatively straightforward.

Yes, I did wonder what I might be getting myself into. I stalled, many times. But something kept pulling me back. Whether you're a natural birth mother, or an adoptive one, it entails a leap of faith, right? There's no warranty that says your child won't have a horrible disease, or become a murderer who will tear out your heart.

I wanted to be bigger than the sum of my weaknesses.

The county adoption agency referred me to a website: www.sundayschild.com.

The first time I went online was a Sunday, appropriately enough.

There's a photo gallery of available children. You click on a child's face, the way you click on an item and put it in your shopping cart.

It's sickening.

Click. You're in a world of lost children.

Click, click. The face fills the screen and stares back at you.

I saw siblings, two boys with damaged eyes, aged nine and thirteen. I worried about them. They'd be hard to place. And sickly looking twins, a boy and girl aged twelve, but they looked way younger. One boy I'm convinced will become a serial killer.

And so on.

But it was Ambrose who spoke to me. He was the youngest—he was only four at the time. He has these long, dark lashes and huge chocolate eyes. Unlike the others, he wasn't smiling in his picture. He looked outraged. I respected him for that: for not being user-friendly and grinning for the camera,

Choose me.

Even his blurb had difficulty putting a gloss over his difficulties.

"Although Ambrose is shy and has developmental issues, he is a great kid and loves to play."

Loves to play.

They said that about every child on the website.

Talitha was beaten senseless by her mother, so she's handicapped now. She loves to play.

Quincy is sixteen and still needs a diaper. He loves to play.

B.J. likes to beat other children.

But he loves to play.

He was abandoned on the restroom floor while his mother turned tricks inside the stall. His mother signed him away for adoption: "He been nothing but trouble." She's in jail now. Murdered someone for a twenty-dollar stash.

Ambrose loves to play.

There's even a photo gallery for prospective parents, the ones still hoping to be matched with a newborn to love and nurture right from the start. Some looked loving and nurturing. Some looked kind of creepy. Some had youth on their side. Some, like me, looked as though they had passed their sell-by dates.

The couples unnerved me.

Their solidarity felt smug, although it probably wasn't. They were probably just about as desperate and insecure as me.

The girl in the shed. You want to know what happened to her.

I found her the morning of Ambrose's first playdate. It had finally stopped raining and it was one of our gorgeous spring mornings. Reese was bringing Cameron over. I was already panicking that the house was a mess, fussing about what to give them to eat, wondering whether it was okay to serve an alcoholic beverage on a playdate.

I didn't know—I'd never had one before.

Then I went to the playhouse to see what state it was in—to check that it hadn't leaked in the rain. It's actually a good space. It was Howard's toolshed once. He put in the heater, the mirror, and a sink for washing tools—and God knows what else.

It's what I said. I didn't ask and he didn't tell.

After he left, I tried to make it nice for Ambrose: I painted it cheery lime, put up jolly posters, had the cupboards built. In truth, it's hardly been used because Ambrose doesn't like being in there alone. If I try to leave him, even for a moment, he follows me out screaming, like he's an extra fleeing a burning building in a disaster movie. It's easier to be with him in the house, where I can cook if I need to, answer the phone. Skim the front page of *The New York Times*, while pretending to play dinosaurs with him.

Don't look so disapproving. If there's one thing I'm capable of, it's getting down on my hands and knees for a good ol' game.

Then I found the girl.

For a moment, I thought she was Ambrose's mother come to claim him, but that was impossible: she'll be away a long time and the girl's hair was too light.

I heard my neighbor's SUV pulling up the street. His name's Greg—or so I've been told by Les, a retired stuntman, who power-walks around the neighborhood all day. I've lived next door to Greg for two years but we've never exchanged a word.

I'd always thought he was an asshole. He built a monster extension, with operatic balconies that look right over my yard. *La-la-la la.* And he has this smug air of prosperity because he's some kind of studio executive.

Well, the studio executives are the ones who put out all the crap that makes billions of dollars, that copies the crap that went before.

Okay, I resent the fact that he's never acknowledged me and he only dates eighteen-year-olds, though he's closer in age to me.

But I didn't resent him so much I wouldn't turn to him.

I ran to him, out onto the street to tell him about the girl in my shed. How I needed help getting her out.

He was sitting in his SUV. He looked rather surprised.

He got out of the vehicle very calmly. He'd just been playing tennis—there was a racket on the front seat, and he was wearing white shorts and a T-shirt. He threw on a Nike jacket (although it was warm) and followed me into the yard to the playhouse. I saw him take a quick glance around. Was probably thinking, *What a dump, but you could do something with the land . . .*

The door was half open, the way I'd left it. I stood to the side, so I couldn't see what was going on, but could hear.

He paused and cleared his throat before knocking, calling in "Hello." Then he leaned on the doorjamb with his head lowered, and his arm slightly bent. The muscle curved up, strong. I wondered if he had a good forearm action.

He waited a moment before trying again, "Hey, look, I'm sorry, but you can't stop in here." His voice was gentle. Too gentle. I was concerned that if he didn't sound tough enough, she wouldn't go.

Then nothing.

She was probably waking up. Coming to . . .

Then I heard her say, "Thank you for not calling the police."

Why did she have to be so friggin' grateful? We were throwing her out!

He answered, "We really don't want to give you a hard time, but there are kids living here. You'll have to move on." Again, he was being so tender and nice.

"Yeah, I see," she replied. "You've got kids, huh?" She assumed Greg was the man of the house.

It makes no sense but I was flattered.

"Yeah."

I was pleased that he lied. It felt protective. Of me, not her.

"What's your name?" she asked.

I wanted to cry, *DON'T TELL HER YOUR NAME!* As if she would become ours forever if he did.

But he said "Greg" very simply, and she replied, "Hey, Greg. Mine's Aurora."

Aurora. It would be.

Then out of respect for her privacy, Greg looked away,

allowing her to gather her things. That was my cue to turn: to look at the orange tree as if there was something going on with the bark. If I'd had a backpack, I would have been buckling it.

I didn't want to see her eyes: they would haunt me if I did.

I heard her—no—*felt* her walking past. I don't know if she saw me and wondered what the lady in the caftan was doing.

When I thought it was safe, I went over to the fence. There's a gap there where a plank's missing—she'd probably squeezed through it in the night.

I used the same opening to watch her go, watch her walk away down the street.

She had a greasy suede bag slung on her shoulder: I remembered seeing it slumped on a chair inside, its tassels now swaying side to side.

Her gait wasn't unhopeful. There was a lightness in her step. She'd had a safe night's sleep and it was a beautiful day.

Again, the back of her head.

Her hair, woven in three coarse strands.

Then she went around the corner and disappeared.

I was left standing with Greg in the yard.

He looked a little dazed.

I didn't know what else to say except *thank you.*

He said *no problem* and gave a tight *no problem* smile that was almost a shrug.

Until then, I hadn't taken in that he was really quite attractive. He has these transparent blue, what are they called? irises, and smooth olive skin, except for a few humorous white lines crinkled around his eyes where the sun can't tan.

I suddenly felt quite emotional.

I can't explain . . . but something inside of me stirred. I hadn't felt anything for a man in so long. I'd forgotten what it was like. It was awkward, because I think he sensed something and didn't know what to do.

Except say goodbye and leave.

Now when I see him, it's a nod of recognition. Like we know something has happened.

But there's no more.

The whole encounter only took five minutes.

I'd left Ambrose up in the house, watching cartoons. I figured he'd be okay for a few more minutes.

I went back to the playhouse.

Saw the blanket, which she'd folded and left on the love seat.

Saw peels on the floor, where she'd eaten an orange from the tree outside.

The radiator was on.

I flicked that off.

I traced her movements from the previous night. Followed the brown drips on the radiator, where she'd devoured the fruit by its warmth, where the juice had dried and darkened as it burned. The blanket, which she'd found, and then went drip, drip, dripping to the sink.

Saw her hairs in the sink: a darker shade of bronze because they were wet.

I pictured her stumbling in the dark, leaning on the sink for support. She never turned on the light. The playhouse is too near the house for her to have risked that.

I saw the small comforts she had taken.

The remnant of an orange.

A child's settee and blanket.

Comforts I denied her.

I never saw her face but I know what it looks like.

It's been haunting me ever since.

It's weathered beyond its years. Too much sun. Not enough light. Her eyes are dead: the vitality's gone. She looks like me. She looks like you. She's the me that, for a roll of the dice, could have ended up like her on the street, dreaming that one day someone would come and rescue me.

We're all one step away from being her.

When I first saw her, I told myself she was dangerous, that I was scared.

When actually I had no fear of *her*, only the terrifying sorrow in myself.

Twenty-two years ago, when life was cheap—abortions were just another form of birth control—I got pregnant. I didn't want the baby. Didn't even think about keeping the baby. So I had it terminated. If that child had lived, the child Jeremy never knew existed, it would have been about the age of the girl in the shed.

After she left, something in me died again.

Ambrose was essentially homeless when I took him in. Why wasn't there room for one more?

That's a question I keep asking myself.

The playdate went well. The experience with Aurora had distracted me so I wasn't thinking about the details.

Everyone ate pizza.

Reese was good company. It turns out she's a research cardiologist, with a specialty in lipids (made the pizza all the more appropriate). She totally unburdened herself about her life as a single mother (the wine I gave her the moment she arrived). But I wasn't really listening.

I was thinking about Aurora.

The boys played. Not together, but side by side. It's the first time I'd seen Ambrose interact with another child in a relaxed, nondefensive way. They built a fort with a wooden set I'd got Ambrose, passing blocks back and forth to each other: bridge to portcullis, block to turret, knight to steed. They built a whole elaborate world. Their collaboration was . . . *perfect.*

I don't want to make too much of this but it was Sunday.

Where does all this leave me?

The things that obsessed me before, whether Ambrose will ever talk, whether he'll get to stay at the Montessori, are worrying me less. I'm more accepting of Ambrose's limitations. Less accepting of mine.

I still worry that I'll be able to stay well and healthy long enough to see Ambrose through.

Until my bones become dry and brittle as an old starfish.

That's what parents are for. Right?

We worry ourselves until death.

But it's hard to look at yourself.

That's why I'm here.

I haven't fixed the fence.

I've been looking for Aurora.

I'd like to think that if I were to see her again, I would stop and ask her if she needed anything. She'd be welcome to stay in the playhouse. There's an air mattress in the garage. I'd get that out, and she could use the bathroom in the house if she wanted.

It's pathetic.
 I know.

LEAVERS' EVENTS

It was the last week of term, the final days being taken up with leavers' events: speeches, concerts and prize-giving, none of which involved Beatty Edwards. In seven years as a senior, Beatty had skirted along the fringes of school life, never integrating into the fabric or fulfilling early predictions of promise. Whereas once she had been the topic of rueful discussion among the more dedicated of her teachers, she was now a subject of terminal interest. Exam results would be revealed on August 17 and her academic future decided. Only the most optimistic of her supporters could still hope to be pleasantly surprised.

Today was the school fete, a fund-raiser hosted by sixth-form parents. The highlight was the raffle, comprising appliances in dog-eared boxes delved from the back of shelves, with the occasional splashy item donated in a gesture of fuck-off generosity. As all sixth-formers were expected to participate, Beatty volunteered to distribute programs: it was quick and painless and meant she could circulate unsupervised. She liked to go at her own pace; to linger at the food stalls for fairy cakes and sausage rolls; potter in the crafts tent, with its funny homespun objects: crochet elephants and rainbow hats for the teapot. While on her rounds, she matched the parents with their offspring: not a difficult task since they all looked like crumpled versions of their daughters. Beatty found it impressive, the commitment with which the mothers manned their stalls. It made her feel less sorry for them that they clearly had nothing better to do with their lives. Beatty knew there was nil chance that her own mother would turn up. She'd long stopped bringing home flyers, seeing her mother push them into the back of drawers. At the first echoes of not too recent Europop distorted over loudspeakers, Beatty found her knapsack and left. The promise of winning an electric skateboard had come four years too late.

Now she was at home, the elaborate flower arrangements that filled the house finally smelled of something. Overnight, with the warm weather, a sultry fragrance pervaded the rooms, creating an atmosphere that seemed to belong somewhere else: a place where people padded in sarongs or lounged in gilded drawing rooms, not a dilapidated house in Hammersmith that had nothing in the fridge.

Her exams over, university applications in, Beatty found her life, so hectic up until now, full of nagging questions. Would it have made much difference if she had worked harder? Was work experience at one of her mother's rival magazines going to be boring or quite interesting? Was she going to get into Edinburgh or Oxbridge, or neither, and then what? Was her boyfriend, Ben, fucking the models who traipsed in and out of the studio clutching their "books"? (Why were they called *books* when they were albums with cuttings from yesterday's magazines?) For years her life had been geared toward these weeks, and now that it was happening, it was not at all what she'd imagined. She had anticipated something more triumphal and significant, instead of a hovering apprehension and a debilitating fatigue. (Was she suffering from a blood disease or simply hungry?)

Beatty drifted through to the kitchen to the refrigerator and hung there on the open door, allowing the cool air to circulate under her armpits. There was never anything in the house that she wanted to eat: none of the diced fruit or roast chicken she saw at other people's houses: cornichons, suppurating cheese, and Dom Perignon were not normal foods—as evidenced from their exclusion from the food pyramid. As if to compound her irritability, today was a dreaded Thursday. Dreaded because Beatty's mother, Vanessa Edwards, the prominent fashion editor, had reserved Thursdays for the family supper. (Vanessa's definition of "family" was strictly limited. It did not include Beatty and Toby's dad, Brian. Charming as he was, he was disqualified by his status as a heroin addict.) Vanessa had instituted these evenings as a way of making up for all the nights when she stayed out late for work. They were mandatory, except when the managing director was in town; then they were promptly canceled. They were always an ordeal—the charade of fifties family dining only seen in films was ludicrous, as was the sight of Vanessa nibbling, rabbit-like, pretending to eat. An argument would always erupt; someone would jerk away from the table and a tear-smudged napkin would be launched in lieu of a missile. Lately, Toby had sensibly eluded these meals. In fact, no one had seen him for days. The last time he'd surfaced he looked like a beaten raccoon. Traditionally, Thursdays were the worst.

The phone was ringing but Beatty didn't answer; she was busy polishing off the last of the Nutella before Gloria, the housekeeper, arrived from the shops and started cooking an indifferent meal. She heard the familiar singsong voice on the answering machine.

"Hel-lo, Iseult here from the office. Your mother's very sorry but she has to cancel, but she has two tickets for *Figaro*—opening night—she thinks you ought to go. Oh, and would you pass this message on to Toby about supper?—if he's there. Bye-ye." *Click.*

A reprieve. *Definitely.* The opera. *Why not?* She liked the costumes and the fantasy of it all.

Except whom should she take?

The obvious candidate was Ben Watts, a photographer's assistant she'd been seeing the last few months, although since the first heated weeks of their relationship, the temperature had steadily dropped. Whereas before he'd found her desirable enough to photograph her naked, the last time they'd slept together he'd teased her about her waistline, laughingly grabbing hold of a roll of fat. (He later claimed he'd been joking, but Beatty was skeptical on the basis that jokes were by intention funny.) Beatty had enough self-respect to know she wasn't fat. Or thin. She was *shapely*. How much she had in common with Ben, she wasn't sure. Ben only talked about work and got suspiciously animated on the subject of her mother, speaking about her in hushed tones reserved for Richard Avedon. When she'd told him about her internship in the accessories department at *Vogue*, "cataloguing knickers," he'd been strangely defensive. "You might learn something."

"Thanks. I've been counting since nursery school." Beatty sniffed.

"You have. That's great," he'd said, clearly not listening.

Ben answered the phone, "Studio." There was always loud music thumping in the background. She didn't know why but that always annoyed her.

"Hello, it's Beatty."

Definitely a disappointed pause.

"Oh, Beatty. What's up?"

"Just wondered if you had plans tonight."

"Yeah. Mmm. I've got to get the cameras ready. We're going on location tomorrow."

"You are?" *Thanks for telling me.* "Where you off to?"

"Bermuda."

Screwing models. "Call me when you get back."

"Right. Mmm . . . take care."

Take care? When did he suddenly become Auntie Ben? It was just as well, she realized—he wouldn't have fit in at a first night. She decided she would find someone suitable, someone worthy of her company. Someone who saw the poetry in things.

Someone like Connor Quinn.

Connor Quinn had only been teaching at the school for a year. At the time his appointment was considered radical: a youngish Irish novelist with literary credentials and little teaching experience, heading the English department at an exclusive girls' school. The Board of Governors had believed that Connor Quinn, a man with just the right amount of notoriety attached to his name, could help shake off an unhelpfully crusty image that the school had accrued in the course of eighty years.

Beatty had taken to Mr. Quinn the moment she'd straggled into his classroom. "Don't rush, Beatty, you're giving me a headache," he'd said without looking up from *The Waste Land*. In advance of their meeting, she'd heard all the talk about his boywonderful career: two novels—gritty memoirs of a terrible Ulster childhood—and his association with a group of other youngish male novelists also known for their precocity. But nothing she'd heard had prepared her for this easygoing charmer of the fallen angel variety. He had sly blue eyes and straight rock-star hair that hung curtain-like and stopped just below his ears. His cheeks were round, perhaps a little puffy. He had his own unique style, delivering lessons while tipping back in his chair and looking at his nails, which were always dirty. She noticed that when she spoke, his eyes crinkled appreciatively and flickered *not just on her face*. During the year, she heard Connor expound on many subjects: art, love, James Joyce's Nora—although she wasn't on the syllabus. All the girls adored Mr. Quinn and fluttered close to his creative flame. The more vigilant parents, noticing the lack of work coming home, wrote letters of complaint to the headmistress, Mrs. Coldstream (she also had a weakness for Connor—fresh air in a school populated by graying female staff). Mrs. Coldstream duly noted their complaints and resolved to fire him once exam results confirmed the worst.

Beatty walked to Connor's flat, which had been pointed out to her by a school friend, much as you would a historic site with a blue plaque. It wasn't far. He lived above a newsagent's near the school. In the distance, she could hear tinny music and voices echoing on the PA, the fete still in progress. But now, by some acoustical trickery, the Continental bistro music sounded like a Muslim call to prayer.

She pushed her note through his letterbox and scurried away as if she had done something furtive—which she had, in a way. Asking a teacher out, even to the opera, was embarrassingly like asking for a date.

It took her half an hour to get home: she'd dawdled on the way.

The phone was ringing when she walked in.

"Mozart. Jonathan Miller. First night. You must be a powerful young lady."

Beatty was taken aback. She hadn't wanted him to be impressed—it was only one of her mum's freebies.

"Does that mean you can't come?"

She heard him laugh and somehow that restored the balance of things. It was nice hearing his voice: its understated, melodic qualities amplified over the phone.

They met in the lobby of the Coliseum. He was smaller than she'd taken in. She realized that when she saw him in class, he was always seated. Or when he stood, she was sitting down. He appeared stockier in a crowd of taller, thinner people. When he saw her, he smiled and slapped her on the back in a friendly sort of way.

The sets were lovely. The singers were unusually attractive and looked as though they had stepped out of a Gainsborough painting. Connor sat very still, occasionally releasing a long sigh of she didn't know what. During the trio, he closed his eyes, seemingly transported by the music. Beatty, all too conscious of his physical presence, tried not to look at him as they sat, except to sneak quick lateral glances out of the corner of her eye. He had an unlikely sanitized smell of medicated soap.

During the intermission they ate sandwiches, dashing Beatty's hopes that they might have gone out to dinner. Connor ordered a whiskey, and Beatty a glass of chardonnay. In truth, Beatty didn't like the sadness and confusion that usually accompanied drinking. She only ordered wine because the occasion seemed to demand it. However, crushed against a window ledge in the bar, eating and drinking with Connor, Beatty experienced none of alcohol's usual muddling effects—only a lighthearted ease. She giggled at Connor's tirade against Wagner's musical verbosity, and nodded vehemently when he confessed to preferring the darker explorations of *Don Giovanni* to the lighter shenanigans of Mozart's other Da Ponte collaborations.

It was raining when they came out. They walked down St. Martin's Lane, jinked toward Charing Cross, where they caught a Number 9 bus, and clambered upstairs. As the bus lurched forward, Connor looked down at Trafalgar Square through the window and said he'd been taken there as a child when his family had come to Britain looking for work. "You can't imagine what an impact coming here made on me and my brother. We climbed on the lions, to the tops of their heads, and looked down on the crowd, the flocks of birds, monochromatic on a dull afternoon. Ma waited below. I was surprised to see her smiling—she didn't seem to mind that we were getting pigeon shite all over our clothes. I tried to fix the moment in my head, to capture a sensation as exalted as any, hoping by force of will I could make it last—when all I was doing was taking a snapshot of our own dismal history."

Beatty listened to Connor with deepening shame. She'd passed the lions a thousand times, never bothering to turn her head at the vermin-infested tourist site. She looked at the lions and saw how monumental and magnificent they must have seemed to Connor and his brother, as they now seemed to her. Until then she hadn't been sure what she wanted out of the evening beyond an interesting diversion, but at that moment, riding high through the darkness with Connor's solid frame by hers, she wanted something to happen between them. For him to move her again and preferably that night.

He walked her to Streatfield Road and stopped outside the front door. She knew she had about twenty minutes before her mother rolled in.

"Would you like a drink?" she asked. Again it seemed like the thing to do.

"Won't we be disturbing your mother?" He didn't say father, so she knew he must have heard about him.

"No, she never gets home before midnight. Don't know how she gets up in the morning."

She did know. Her mother had a ritual that involved inverting for thirty minutes with cold compresses strapped to her face. (Heaven forbid if anyone disturbed her before eight.) Then she drank the vinegar water, did the makeup, put on her trademark round black glasses that made her look like a twenties swimmer. Ray, her driver, picked her up at nine.

They went into the sitting room and Connor looked around. There wasn't much to look at, almost nothing on the walls since her dad had pilfered nearly everything. It was the same with the furniture. It had been a slow disappearing act, one piece at a time, so you almost didn't notice something had gone. Fortunately he had left the sofa, on which Connor was about to sit.

"Nice place," he said, sinking into the ivory linen cushions. "Uncluttered."

She loved him for saying that.

Beatty looked around for something to drink. She could have sworn there was some whiskey somewhere. In her nerves she forgot about the champagne in the fridge. All she could find was some murky liquid in a decanter.

"I'm afraid this has been here for ages."

Connor nodded. "Vintage something. I'll take it."

Beatty poured them both a glass and passed him one. He was the first to taste.

"I think it's Madeira, my dear-a," Connor said, swilling it in his mouth.

She followed with a gulp, which felt like heat rushing to her brain. She was still standing, feeling the dizzying effects of the Madeira, when she noticed Connor looking at her. His eyes seemed to be boring into her, quite different from his back-slapping demeanor at the Coliseum.

Here we go.

"Come here," he said, as if on cue.

She trotted over to him and perched foolishly on his knee, before he pulled her down into his lap and kissed her—such a relief he was finally taking charge. He had nice lips: soft, like jelly, and a strong, probing tongue. He said something about her being lovely, which made her flush and think of Ben. All the while, she had a thrilling out-of-body disbelief that she was snogging Mr. Quinn, at the same time imagining herself telling selected friends. Now he was slowly unbuttoning her blouse, saying, "You know, I don't consider you my student anymore." She knew what he meant: there were no more lessons, only the winding down of it all. She straddled him now. It felt *good*, asserting herself. He was hard and she could feel him pressing up underneath. He pushed his hand inside her skirt, fingers slipping purposefully under her knicker elastic. Between quickening breaths, she said—as he'd brought up the subject—"I might be staying on next term to do Oxbridge."

She felt him stiffen.

"Is that a fact?"

She was hurt he sounded so surprised—it wasn't inconceivable she could get in. Or maybe he was annoyed that she hadn't filled him in. "I was talking to Miss Marsden about doing History. She thinks it's a possibility, subject to the results, of course. I'd prefer to do English, but I don't think my grades are going to be good enough. I mean, I didn't even finish the last essay on Pope." She hoped he wouldn't take that as a criticism: it was true History was a stronger option due to the fact they'd completed the syllabus.

They had now drawn apart—it wasn't the sort of conversation that happened up close. He ran his fingers through his hair. His eyes had lost their approving crinkle. They now looked . . . tired. She realized that her doing Oxbridge was some sort of impediment to their having sex.

He took one last slug on his drink and said, "Thanks for the opera," before going home, she presumed, to his flat.

Lying in bed, with a sinking knowledge that she had handled things badly, Beatty heard the halting clicks of Vanessa's pinnacle heels downstairs in the hall. Beatty felt furious with her. Through some convoluted late-night thinking, she attributed the failure of the evening to her mother's existence in the world. She felt like going down and telling her as much, but she knew at that time of night it was the equivalent of pushing a toddler in the playground.

Besides, she didn't feel so well.

Then, she threw up the egg sandwich Connor had bought her in the interval.

The vomiting continued through the night. Her mother, hearing her groans, came teetering in with towels and a wastepaper basket. Beatty's initial thought was that the Madeira hadn't agreed with her. But when the sickness continued two more days, accompanied by a raging temperature and mumpish swelling, the doctor came and diagnosed glandular fever.

Beatty stayed in bed for two weeks and missed the last days of term. Her mother arranged for little boxed foods from Selfridges to be delivered, which Gloria reheated and brought up to her room. She half expected a visit from Mr. Quinn, imagining their meeting in her bedroom, lovers in the last act of *La Bohème*. Failing that, she at least expected a bunch of flowers or a thoughtful little note.

But nothing came.

He probably caught the wretched thing himself.

Her only visitor from school was her unlikely friend Louise. Louise was a hearty achiever, a shoo-in for Oxford. Beatty had always admired Louise's impossibly cheerful ambition and hoped one day some of it would rub off on her. After delivering grapes and opening all the windows, Louise sat down on Beatty's bed and launched into an account of the last teary telephone-number-swapping, flower-giving days of school. Beatty listened patiently and could barely wait to ask her question.

"Has Mr. Quinn been absent?"

"No. I saw him today," Louise replied.

The week Beatty graduated *in absentia*, her mother was offered the editorship of an American magazine. It was a coup, but it meant she had to leave suddenly for New York to a *funereal* brownstone

91

off University Place, which she promptly swapped for a *non-depressing* one. Toby stayed behind to study for the retakes of January's retakes and to "house-sit." Beatty followed on three weeks later when she was well enough to travel.

It was ninety-five degrees when Beatty arrived at JFK and stepped onto the steaming tarmac and got immediately stuck in a bottleneck of trollies driven by half-crazed people. The melee struck Beatty as near-miraculous: the manic energy spoke to her inner turmoil; her as-yet-unreleased creativity. She knew she had found a place where she would be understood—that could take her by surprise, and for everything she had.

Beatty was given a job working as a fashion assistant at her mother's magazine, even though the department was already fully staffed by impeccable android-like young women who were in awe of Beatty's slovenly habits and position as daughter of the editor. Rather than conform to their impossible ways, Beatty cultivated her own chaotic charms as a way to diffuse the competition, create goodwill, and give her more leeway in which to operate. Her clothes became increasingly outlandish (black lace mantilla in the morning) so that they were a daily source of humor and comment in the office. She realized her metamorphosis from dumpy school-girl to "English eccentric" was better than going unnoticed, the equivalent of career-cancer in her profession.

By the end of the summer, Beatty hadn't even bothered to call Toby to get her exam results (he never answered the phone anyway), Edinburgh/Oxbridge were way off her radar. She was too busy—hooked on her new life. Her days were spent traipsing around photographers' studios, arms filled with clothes to adorn preternaturally endowed girls. Her nights, doing the rounds of restaurants and clubs. Within a year she was given her own office (*so what if it was a shoe box?*), a newly created job title (*Associate*

Fashion Editor-at-Large), and, more important, someone to do the traipsing for her.

Beatty discovered that she and her mother had a new cord to bind them: the magazine. She felt empathy for Vanessa, seeing her embattled as she tried to stem the damage of declining circulation. The stresses of her mother's life were painfully apparent, from her emaciated body to the liverish shadows under her eyes that no bottles of discreet makeup could conceal.

That was before her mother went and had the surgery.

During the four weeks' "holiday" when her mother was out of the office, Beatty sensed a change in the air. It could be felt in the way a memo was dumped on her desk, or a knowing look received in the corridor. Finally it was left to a colleague in Human Resources to tell Beatty her mother was about to be shafted by the assistant editor, but she needn't worry because Beatty was liked and was going to be asked to stay on.

The day Vanessa was due back, Beatty arranged a lunch with her mother at the Four Seasons: a way of giving moral support before the axe was dropped on Vanessa's sadly rearranged head. Beatty was at her desk. Clio, her assistant, had just come in with contact sheets and her hourly mineral water. There was an uncharacteristic lull in the day, and Beatty had a moment to reflect on how unlikely her life had become. Unlikely to the point of foreignness. Unlikely to the point of it being *sort of fucking scary*. She suddenly flashed on Connor and had an urge to talk to him, to tell him what she'd been doing. For him to be surprised, even a little impressed, and then for him to make her laugh about it. Any residual embarrassment about the dismal anticlimax of their last evening together had faded. They were both grown-ups now. The last she'd heard of him was in a postcard from Louise (loving St. Margaret's) who'd written, "P.S. Heard C.Q. has been fired!"

Beatty still had Connor's number. When Clio updated her address book, Beatty had made sure it was transcribed. She'd had a feeling she'd one day need it again.

While Beatty listened to the quaintly familiar *ring-ring* of British Telecom, she suddenly had a stabbing thought that Connor might have met someone. If he had, Beatty sincerely hoped she wouldn't answer the telephone. For a moment, she envied her putative rival. She wouldn't have minded him for herself. Beatty's recent encounters had been with boys who loved boys, or girls who only liked girls pretending to be boys. The thought of retiring with Connor (bohemian London couple) away from the Darwinian unpleasantness suddenly seemed rather appealing.

And then Connor picked up.

God, he's there!

"Hello," he said, voice husky with sleep.

Beatty quickly checked the time difference. *No, five hours forward is five in the afternoon there . . .*

"Connor. It's Beatty Edwards here." She held her breath, waiting for a roar of recognition and that infectious laugh of his.

"What?" He sounded gruff.

It must be a bad line.

She tried upping her voice. "It's Beatty—Beatty Edwards." She heard a pause. Then a transatlantic crackle of phlegm.

"Who the fuck's that?"

Beatty stared at the receiver, unable to find an answer.

There was a horrible silence, punctuated by rustling at his end.

He doesn't know who I am.

Then, *click.* He hung up.

Beatty dropped the phone back into the receiver. It was a stunning, ego-defying moment. And then her mind filled with justifications: she must have caught him at a difficult moment—*an extremely bad one*; he'd just received news of a death in the family—

he'd said something about a sister being alive; or maybe since losing his job, he'd fallen on hard times—*that can't be easy.*

She unstopped the bottle, pouring water into her glass.

He doesn't remember.

She continued pouring. The water flowed over the sides, forming an effervescent puddle on the pale chrome of her desk. Beatty stared at the water, imagining him unemployed in his flat over the newsagent's. Was he even attempting to work or had he given that up as well? She realized that she'd never asked him why he'd stopped writing in the first place. She remembered how his fingers felt inside her. The thought of it still made her face burn.

Her cell phone started ringing. She could see by the number it was Randy, her driver, come to pick her up.

She took one last look at the silvery pool that seemed to hold an imperfect vision of the past; it would disperse mercury-like if touched, as if it had never been there at all. And then she banished Connor Quinn, replacing him with more pressing thoughts.

Such as lunch—which she was dreading—but at least the spa menu promised to be good.

She found her purse and clip-clopped out of her office.

The bubbles fizzed and popped, and eventually disappeared.

BABY
CHARMER

WEDNESDAY, MARCH 6

The agency called this morning and I had only a couple of hours to get myself ready. My lucky interview jacket had a stain on the lapel, so I ran around like a maniac, dabbing and sponging, but I think I looked presentable enough when the time came. The client's name is Mrs. Powers. The agency said she's married to the film director Marty Powers. Who is he? I'll only look him up if I'm hired.

The family live miles up in the hills. It's a huge property, surrounded by other huge properties—all high fences and security cameras. Mrs. Powers is attractive, with soft honey highlights. She's lost all her baby weight already and seemed pleased when I said so. We interviewed in the library.

Do you smoke?
    No. Filthy habit.

———

Approach to discipline?
  Caring reinforcement of values.

Seven years at your last job. That's a long time.
  Yes it is.

She didn't say anything—so I added, The mum decided to spend some time at home and Tyler was at school full-time, blah, blah, blah. I skip the part that Mum never around. Tyler stopped talking to Mum. Mum not too happy about that . . .

She wonders whether I'm familiar with breastfeeding techniques. I ask whether the agency has perhaps forgotten to send my résumé. She shuffles through her papers. *Oh, here it is. Lactation specialist and a nursing diploma.* I needed her to know that she has to do her homework too. We touched upon salary and I tell her I need my health insurance paid. She didn't bat an eyelid and said that sounded reasonable, which surprised me. That's usually when the attitude changes and they say they'll have to talk to their husbands. She seemed nice so I'm keeping my fingers crossed. Good families are hard to come by.

Stopped by Zora's to warn her that I might need her to look after Tabs again—hope I'm not jinxing anything. Zora threw her head back and laughed. She thinks it's a joke because Tabs is looked after by the entire building, and goes from door to door like he's starving and he's getting fatter by the minute. I know that Bob in 9C is still feeding him even though I asked him not to, and lied to my face, *I wouldn't dream of doing such a thing,* when I've actually seen Tabby climbing out his window with prosciutto hanging from his mouth. He's reeking of cologne and he has his neck fur fluffed forward. I want to take one of Tabby's turds and shove it up Bob's waste disposal. Excuse me. I didn't write that . . .

Zora's place was the usual mess and stinks. I've told her you can't just stuff the nappies in the Diaper Genie and leave them to rot. You have to change the canister from time to time. She was complaining about Mrs. Sanchez from the first floor, how she's always late to pick up Carlos because she can't leave the kid she looks after because the mum is also late from work. That kind of behavior makes me sick. I don't know why you'd have a kid if you can't look after it. I don't know how Zora will manage when her children have to be in school. And it's only a matter of time before she finds herself in trouble for running a daycare without a permit.

Was just making myself some Pot Noodle when the phone rang. I closed my eyes and I say a little prayer. I pick up the phone and hear Helena saying, "You've got the job, hon, subject to background checks. You'll have to sign a confidentiality clause because the family's in the business." The clause is no problem. I'm used to that. As if anyone would be interested in their dirty little secrets.

THURSDAY, MARCH 7

No news. Still waiting to hear about the job. I try to stop myself getting excited in case it doesn't come through. In the meantime I'm spring-cleaning my flat, and having the usual battle with myself about my storage. I hate the wire racks in my bedroom with all my clothes and intimates on display. No matter how much you fold, it always manages to look messy. I consider having closets built, with drawers and railings that swish in and out and all my clothes arranged in sections, and then I think *why bother?* I'll only be improving the apartment for the landlord. I should save my money for when I finally go back home to England.

FRIDAY, MARCH 8

I decided to get my roots done professionally as a treat to myself. On my way out to the salon, I pass Bob in the hall. I flash him my nicest smile and he looks at me as if I'm the devil. You can't win with these people.

Melinda did a nice job with my hair. It's softer. Less brassy than before. I look quite posh.

SATURDAY, MARCH 9

The family must have lawyers working overtime. Helena called to say I've been cleared to work and they want me to start immediately. Now I can relax and get myself organized. I'm looking forward to it, even though I know there's always an adjustment period, and there's always compromises to be made. I packed my bag and laid out my clothes for the morning: floral skirt with a light cable pullover and scarf. It reminded me of the night before primary school when I set my uniform on the floor: blouse, tunic, knickers, even hair elastics. It looked like an effigy of me—until Mum stumbled through it on one of her rants. But I like the feeling of new beginnings, even the butterflies in my stomach.

BABY CHARMER

Mrs. Powers looked a bit rough when I arrived—a few nights looking after your own kid will do that to you. She was friendly enough and showed me my room. It's quite large, with built-in closets and decorated with florals. We both looked at my skirt, then at the walls, and had a good old chuckle together because they matched. The room is next to the baby's—of course—but it has its own en-suite, television, and DVD. I told her that I was against TV for the little one, especially now the experts have "discovered" what we've known for ages—that television is bad for children—but said that I wouldn't promise not to watch it myself. When she asked me what I liked to watch, I told her the Sci-Fi channel—she looked at me as if I'd stepped off of a flying saucer!

The baby's a good 'un but he's not on a schedule. Mrs. Powers said he's only done one five-hour stretch and that was at 11:00 p.m. a few weeks ago and they all leaped up and down but he's not done it since. It's amazing the money people pay for a baby nurse, and you arrive and the baby doesn't know what it's doing, and everyone's miserable because no one's sleeping, but you're the one who has to pick up the pieces—and they're paying you a quarter of what they wasted on the baby nurse because you're only the nanny. I know I'm ranting, but this is what it's for. To get it all out.

The baby's name is Zachary but they call him Zak.

———

6:00 p.m. Sat with Mum while she expressed milk—she talked about the shameful lack of lactation support for new mothers. She's seriously into the whole La Leche, breast-milk-only thing. I gave Zak a bath and feed, and he went straight to sleep. He's adorable. I can see he's going to be no trouble at all. Then Mrs. Powers takes me along the corridor and shows me the upstairs kitchenette, "In case you get hungry in the night"—her way of saying they don't want to see me downstairs past six. They think they're being so subtle, when they might as well put a sign: PISS OFF WHEN WE DON'T NEED YOU.

I say, *Ooh, you've got all my favorites—Pot Noodle, baked beans, and Marmite. How did you guess?*

I'm thinking, I'll be farting like a trooper.

Met Dad for a moment. He's a lot older than her with silver hair and a gravelly voice. With his smooth, tanned skin and his large white teeth, he looks like a Hollywood movie star or a former president. He passed me in the hall and said, "Glad to have you on board," which was nice and set me at ease.

I woke Zak up at 11:00 p.m., gave him his last feed and change, and put him down to sleep.

MONDAY, MARCH 11

Zak woke up at 6:15—that's a seven-hour stretch already.
When I came in, he smiled at me, bless him. I think his eyes are going to stay blue. They're just like Dad's.

Inez, the housekeeper, arrived at five past nine. I made sure I was friendly to her. The housekeepers can give you trouble if you get on their wrong side—especially if they've worked there a long time. I asked her about her children. She has four in El Salvador but she and her husband live here. I got the impression, just a look in her eye, that she does all the work and her husband's useless and doesn't pull his weight in the family. Inez shot straight into the baby's room, checking up on my hygiene habits. That's what gets them the most—nannies that make them do all the dirty work and treat them like they're the help. I know she noticed right away that the room was immaculate. There's nothing festering in my Diaper Genie. Inez lives-in only when the family travel. It's unusual, a family like them not having a live-in—they must really be in love with their privacy. When I asked Inez about her hours, she got cagey, as if I was asking a state secret. I didn't push it because it's only a matter of time before she'll be telling me everything down to the fact she's not paying taxes and asking whether she should ask for a raise.

Mrs. Powers asked me to keep the pump set up so it's ready for her, while she does this and that, before she goes out. She must be seeing a trainer, because she went out in a hoodie and sweatpants, and came back flushed a few hours later. She was pleased when I told her about Zak's long stretch.

TUESDAY, MARCH 12

Saw Mr. Powers leave this morning. He must be going away for a while since he had a lot of luggage. (Maybe he's making a film?

Mrs. Powers hasn't said anything.) She saw him off in her dressing gown. Her head was dropped low so I couldn't tell if she was sad. He kissed her on the forehead before he went.

Mum came down again at 9:30. She'd pumped and wanted Zak. She took him out onto the terrace and sat on a swinging settee, cooing at him. I was glad when she gave him back that he was still awake. If he'd slept that early, it would have thrown him for the rest of the day.

WEDNESDAY, MARCH 13

Zak slept straight through for seven hours last night, which is great for a little fella. I told Mrs. Powers and she was delighted and said she hoped he'd be as obliging for her on the weekend.

Before Mrs. Powers went off, I asked about local parks. She blinked and said that there was one at the bottom of the glen but there was a nice play area around the back of the house—maybe I hadn't seen it—and she was going to put in a climbing set sometime soon. I agreed that was a great idea, and told her for sure we'd enjoy the benefit of their stunning home, but I also said it was important for Zak to have some social interaction outside the house. For example, he could be enrolled in a music course, or baby gymnastics, or even some "Mommy and Me" classes. Mrs. Powers seemed a bit put out, and said she wasn't comfortable with anyone apart from herself driving Zak—that she'd do all the driving to doctor's appointments, etc. (we'll see how long that lasts). I couldn't argue with her, her being the mum. So I held my tongue—for now anyway.

6:30 p.m. Put Zak to bed, snoozed on and off while I watched TV. At 10:30 I got up, did another feed and change, put him down, and went back to bed. At around 11:00, I heard Mrs. Powers going in. She spent about ten minutes in there, murmuring. (Hope to God she's not picking him up. Don't want him getting any bad habits off her.) After that, I heard her feet stopping outside my door. I was actually dozing, but as I'm used to rousing at the slightest sound, I woke up and wondered what she was listening for. The clink of gin bottles? Or is she trying to catch me yakking about her to my boyfriend? Thankfully there's no chance of that. Last thing I need is another baby to look after.

THURSDAY, MARCH 14

This morning Mrs. P. went out and came back three hours later in a blind panic—she'd got stuck in traffic and thought there wasn't enough milk for Zak's feed. I calmed her and told her there was sufficient—there was still two ounces backup in the freezer as I'd frozen the excess the night before. She looked surprised. She didn't seem to know it was okay to freeze breast milk. I assured her it was fine, as long as you followed some commonsense guidelines, i.e., you only freeze when it's fresh and you don't wait until it's curdling in the fridge. Seeing how she worked herself into a state reminded me how hard breastfeeding is on a woman. But it's such a personal matter that I never intervene and I never give advice. Women get so touchy on the subject, as if their whole sense of motherhood is dependent on how much milk they're producing, when supplementing formula is fine—little ones need something heavier to sustain them through the night. A hungry baby is not a contented one.

ETHER

It's Friday already. The week has gone by quickly. I'm to stay until Saturday morning, then I'm off until 8:00 a.m. Monday—that's to give Mrs. Powers the feeling that she's looked after the baby the entire weekend! Inez is now working Saturdays, a six-day week. She was only half complaining because she's glad of the money and she says there's nothing for her at home with her children being so far away.

SATURDAY, MARCH 16

I'm glad to get home. Even though everyone talks about my stamina, it's not what it used to be. I don't have that extra bounce in the morning. The moment I get in, I change into my jim-jams. There was a time when I would have put on my leggings and joined the unemployed hordes, powering up the canyons, but now, frankly, I can't be bothered. Who cares if I've got a wobbly backside?

SUNDAY, MARCH 17

After breakfast (bliss, Frosted Flakes in front of the TV), I went down the hall. Zora's a mess. She's flat out on the sofa while the kids are in the kitchen making dough balls, and there's flour everywhere. Somehow they've managed to get it on the ceiling. I make Zora some tea, while she starts again on the tardiness of the mums. I tell her she should charge overtime, that would stop them from being late. But she says she hasn't the heart and no one can afford to pay extra anyway. She asks me about becoming a nanny, whether she could try doing what I do. But I had to be tough with her. I told her that anyone can call themselves a nanny, but what matters is experience and the letterhead on your references. A nursing diploma counts a lot, so does speaking proper English and being able to drive. I explained that people didn't like hiring ladies with small children because it makes them unreliable: they rush home to their kids at the first sign of a fever. I've interviewed with people who start clapping when I say I'm single, no kids, and no intention of having them. My best advice to her was to wait until the kids are in school, then I'd help her get a cleaning job, somewhere in the Beverly Hills flats where she can use public transport and she won't need a car.

MONDAY, MARCH 18

Arrive back at work—to my horror Mrs. Powers is talking on the phone while Zak is napping in an electric bassinette/swing, the equivalent of giving the baby Valium. I hate those things. The motion makes the baby nod off but soon it's addictive. Soon they'll only sleep if they're rocked—which is fine for the first weeks, but a few months down the line when you've got a strapping twenty-pounder, your back is killing you from all that rocking, and the baby now wakes up as soon as it realizes you've stopped. I'll wait one more day to tell Mrs. Powers. Then I'm getting rid of that contraption, even if she only got it in on the weekend.

The moment Mrs. Powers is off the phone, she says she's had a bad weekend because Zak woke up every two hours during the night wanting to feed. She can't understand it. He'd been doing so well—but no lovely long stretches for her. She says she's in awe of me. That I must be some kind of baby charmer. I tell her not to worry. Children always act up for their parents. It's just the way it is. She looked alarmed at first, before she smiled and asked me what I'm doing for the next twenty years.

I like Mrs. Powers. I think I'm going to be happy here.

TUESDAY, MARCH 19

Zak was cranky—he's definitely off his routine and fussed instead of napping after lunch. It was a beautiful day. I took him out in the sling and we walked around the garden and watched hummingbirds, flitting about like fairies. The garden has a citrus grove and an area planted with cactuses, and palms with brilliant flowers shooting up like exotic birds. Even in the sunshine, I found myself thinking about Mum in England. She's probably alone, sitting by the window, looking out at the rain. Serves her bloody right. WHERE'S YOUR BOYFRIEND NOW? I want to scream.

Managed to get in six episodes out of the Trekkie marathon, with William Shatner, not the bald one who looks like a part of the male anatomy. That wasn't my line—it's from the chat room where everyone was fighting over the captains. Shatner versus The Bald One (one of the nicer comments). I have to agree with kirklover@ bigfoot.com that the captain of the Starship Enterprise cannot be someone you want to sleep with. He has to be someone that you trust.

WEDNESDAY, MARCH 20

What did I say? While Zak was sleeping, I went into the laundry room and Inez comes in. She corners me and for the next forty minutes she tells me everything: about every little Christmas present the Powers have ever given her, and every single bonus. She says she likes working for Mrs. Powers but wants to know whether I think she should ask for a car because hers is old and giving her trouble. I listen, thinking, *that's a bit steep.* I'd never ask for a car. I prefer to get my money up front and figure out my own expenses. Suddenly, I see Mrs. Powers walking past with Zak in her arms. Zak is crying because he's obviously just woken up hungry and wants his lunch, and I hadn't heard because the intercom was out of range. But then I see Mrs. Powers's face—she's glaring at me as if I'm a criminal, when I know he can only just have woken up because it wasn't wake-time before then. I follow Mrs. Powers into the kitchen where she's sitting in the wicker rocker, breastfeeding— a first at that time of day. (She must really be trying to make a point!) So I put the kettle on and say, He can't have been awake long. (In such a way it could be a question.)

She replied, *Long enough. I don't want him left crying like that again.*

I had to say, Don't worry, he won't be.

Meanwhile, I'm thinking, Inez should ask for a car. Then she'll see what Mrs. Powers is really made of.

THURSDAY, MARCH 21

Now Zak is sleeping better at night, he's more alert in the day and wants stimulating. At my suggestion, we went to the Small Wonder Learning Center and bought him all the latest educational toys. After, we had lunch in a café. Mrs. Powers was reserved at first, but loosened up by the time the coffee came. It turns out she

ETHER

was an actress once, but she got shy when I asked her what she'd been in, and she said she was glad to be out of the rat race. If I can find out her maiden name, maybe I'll look her up and find out why she went so red.

FRIDAY, MARCH 22

The week has gone by quickly. Zak's on track with his sleeping. He loves his new play mat and lies there flexing his little drumsticks, and he's really trying to reach up and touch his reflection in the dangly mirror. I keep telling Mrs. Powers that he's powerful for his age—that he'll be a bodybuilder and governor before long. I've been doing flash cards with him. Mrs. Powers seemed glad about that. I'm sure she's thinking, *rather her than me.*

SATURDAY, MARCH 23

This morning I was cutting Zak's nails on the changing table (my least favorite job, sets my teeth on edge—must be something to do with sharpies near tender flesh) when Inez comes in and says it hasn't gone well with Mrs. Powers about the car. Mrs. Powers told her that she already paid way over the fair salary and should try to make do with what she was driving. Inez was very upset. She seemed angry with me for suggesting it—charming, when I was only looking out for her interests. I tell her that there's no way she's getting paid over the rate. Given the length of time she'd been working there, I would expect someone of her caliber to be getting at least another hundred bucks a week. You should have seen Inez's eyes balloon. You could practically see dollar signs in them. Then I went into the kitchen to put the bottles in the sterilizer. Mrs. Powers was on the telephone. When I came in she suddenly stopped talking and rang off quickly. It made me

112

exceedingly uncomfortable. I could only think of two reasons why she'd do that.

One: she's talking to someone else, the *someone* she sees in the morning who isn't Mr. Powers.

Two: she was talking about me.

Glad I'm going home this afternoon.

WEEKEND ENDING MARCH 24

I didn't write this weekend. Was in such a hurry to leave on Saturday—everyone seemed to be in a bad mood—that I left my bag at the house. A real bummer as it has my whole life in it. So I'm actually writing this on Monday. I realized that this is only the second time since I was seventeen that I've missed an entry for more than one day.

Not much to report. Saw Zora. Went to the mall and bought myself a hoodie in the Robinson's sale. It's not really my style, but it will be useful for exercising. I'm thinking of taking it up again. It might make me feel better.

MONDAY, MARCH 25

I arrived back at the house a little early and went straight to the kitchen. I see Mrs. Powers on the phone and Zak is on the terrace, napping in the contraption, and figure they must have had another bad night for him to be sleeping so early. As I didn't want to interrupt one of her *private* conversations, I slipped upstairs to catch up on the weekend.

TUESDAY, MARCH 26

I'm writing this from home.

Yesterday, after I finished my diary, I went downstairs—bang on the dot of 8:00—no one can say I'm not punctual. On the way down, I ran into Inez with her arms full of sheets.

I'm surprised she's there that early and think Zak must have been sick on the weekend and Mrs. P. asked her to stay.

But when I say, Good morning Inez, she didn't answer.
     And when I asked her how her Sunday was, she looked away.

I go back to the kitchen. Mrs. Powers is off the phone. She's sitting at the breakfast bar, big bags under her eyes. She says she needs to talk to me.

I smile, and say, Of course. And I sit down opposite her.

This isn't working. I feel you're not happy here.

114

BABY CHARMER

I'm stunned.

I say, I don't know what might have given you that impression.

She says, *If you're honest with yourself you know it's true.*

My throat's tight. No words come out.

You know what I'm talking about.

I'm not sure what she's getting at, so I try, If you want me to leave, I'll go.

Yes. That would be the best thing to do.

So I get up and smile again. I'll be damned if she sees me cry.

I'll just get my things.

Then she adds: *By the way, I don't appreciate you trying to make Inez leave.*

———

I stop.

I *never* tried to make Inez leave.

She says, *Inez told me. Who do you think I'm going to believe? Someone I've known for eight years, or someone I've just met?*

I can't believe Inez. The backstabbing bitch. Mrs. Powers has made up her mind, so there's no point arguing.

Could I say goodbye to Zak?

She hesitates before saying, *Yes*.

She follows me to the patio. Zak is slumped in the swing, sleeping. He looks like a crumpled angel. I lean down and kiss him on the forehead.

Goodbye. God bless.

I go up to my room. It doesn't take me long to pack. There's not much there.

Mrs. Powers waits downstairs in the hall. I pass her on my way out to the car. Don't look at her. Just put my chin up and keep walking.

The door closes behind me.

Just as I'm going to the car, I hear the door opening again. I turn and see it's Mrs. Powers. As if she can't help herself, she's following me out. I hurry to the car, slam the door shut—not exactly in the mood for conversation. I'm fiddling with the keys, trying to get them in the ignition.

Mrs. Powers is at my window.

She leans in and hisses, *I know why he isn't sleeping when you're not here.*

I don't wait for the rest. I accelerate away as fast as I can.

Back at home, once I've calmed myself, my second call is to Helena to tell her how Mrs. Powers is impossible—that I couldn't stay there a moment longer, even though I felt terrible about leaving that poor child. Helena listens—could tell she wasn't at all happy about the situation—and said she'll need to hear what Mrs. Powers has to say before she sets up any other interviews for me. To top it all, I open my bag and there's powder everywhere. The lid from the container must have worked itself off, and there's formula all over my clothes: it's in my hairbrush, clogging my toothbrush, these pages. Everywhere. I'll never get it out.

WEDNESDAY, MARCH 27

Couldn't sleep, thinking about the lies Mrs. Powers will tell Helena. I might tell Helena about the formula so she fully understands the situation—how Mrs. Powers's breast milk was dishwater because she never eats, how the baby couldn't sleep because he was half-starved. As for Inez, my only comfort is that the next nanny will treat her the way she deserves, and the Powerses will chew her up and spit her out when they're through. There's no such thing as loyalty with people like that. They all pretend that you're part of their happy family, but really you're just as disposable as a full nappy.

THURSDAY, MARCH 28

Another bad night. More fretting. Helena called first thing. Mrs. Powers has refused to talk about what went on. Her only explanation was: *Let's just say I'm really in love with my privacy.* Helena asks me what I think she meant by that. At first I can't answer, I'm so upset. I take a deep breath and say, "I think Mrs. Powers is having some personal problems—you know, with her marriage. She's a little unbalanced," which seemed to satisfy Helena because she lets rip on Mrs. Powers. Apparently Mrs. Powers has had the nerve to ask for her commission back and said she will never use the agency again! I've never heard Helena so angry. She's letting me interview on the weekend, which is great. For the first time in days, I fall asleep sitting up on the settee.

BABY CHARMER

FRIDAY, MARCH 29

Feeling better today. Must have slept about twenty hours. I was having lunch—chicken-rice—when I heard a knock at the door. I found Zora in the corridor crying because she's had a visit from the City—someone reported her. They've cited her and closed her down. I commiserate, telling her to look on the bright side. It was high time she sat down to take stock of her life. And I really meant it. What did she expect?—I was doing her and those poor kids a favor when I made that call.

SATURDAY, MARCH 30

The night before my interview, I can't help thinking about Zak. I hope my replacement is nice for his sake—although there's only so much a nanny can do. He'll probably end up on Prozac just like his mother. As for her, hope she's stewing over the fact that her fancy lawyers were too busy to send over the confidentiality agreement.

I lay out my outfit for tomorrow. This time there's no stain on the lapel to spoil my luck. The family live in Pasadena, a lovely place. I went there to a flea market once, when I was first setting up my apartment. I know it's silly but I have butterflies.

I'm looking forward to seeing what tomorrow may bring.

119

CAREFUL
MUMMY

Mummy, were you ever scared when you were a little girl?"

"Yes, of course, darling." *Shitless.* "All children get frightened sometimes."

"What were you scared of?"

Keep it light but plausible. "Well, we lived in a big, drafty old house, not a nice cozy one like this, and there was this silly television program with things called Daleks and Cybermen and I thought they were frightening when they weren't at all." *I'd lie awake, rigid, at the top of the house—so when "Uncle Clive" came in I was actually quite glad to see him.* "What are you scared of?"

"Monsters."

"Lobsters?"

"Nooo. Monsters."

"I've been around a long time and I've never seen a monster. And my mummy never saw a monster," *she shut her eyes when she married him,* "or my mummy's mummy," *she was the beast herself, or so the story goes.* "So I think we can safely say that monsters don't exist."

There, that wasn't badly done.

"Are you going to die one day?"

What do I say? What do I say? Making it taboo only heightens the dread. "Yes, as a matter of fact, one day I will."

"Aahhh!"

ETHER

God, the face—too young for the truth. The size of her tears. They're almost voluptuous. "But it won't be for a very, very long time and I'll only go when you don't need me anymore." *That's right. Fill her with promises you can't keep.* "Look here, in my eyes. I'm not going anywhere. I promise." *At least she's stopping . . .*

"Are you going to get gray hair?"

"Yes. Sure I will."

"Ahhhh!"

I should have said, no I'm going two shades darker. "Please, darling. It's nothing to worry about." *She's truly horrified. Is repulsion for the aged primal and not conditioned?* "I'll tell you what. When the time comes I'll wear a wig." *At last. A smile. She kills me.*

"So when I get to be your age, what's going to happen to you?"

Good question.

"I mean do you shrink like you're in the washing machine?"

Well, yes, actually. "Well, yes, actually. You clever little girl." *I was clever once.* "I love you so much." *I don't deserve you. Or you, me.*

"I love you too, Mummy."

"That makes me so very happy."

"Then why are you crying?"

"I am not."

"Yes, you are. There, in your corners. I've caught you!"

They'll deliver if I call now. "Don't be silly." *Twenty should be enough.* "It must be the light—or the dark . . . I'm just going to make a quick telephone call."

"Can I have a story?"

"I'll be back in a minute."

"You always say that. Can I have a story later?"

"I'll see . . ." *Fuck. That hurt. Who put that chair there?*

"What happened? Did you hurt yourself? Careful, Mummy."

ETHER

They met at a nice restaurant near her office. They ate grilled sole with tender vegetables and drank a decent bottle of wine. She tactfully measured the progress of his new work. He managed to conjure an impression that whatever he'd write next would be a credit to them both. Fucking afterward had not been inevitable. That depended on his performance at lunch; whether he'd been able to make her chuckle with a well-turned barb, make those stubborn eyebrows of hers widen and rise. Vivian Newman was no pushover. She was educated and smart. Vivian ran marathons in her spare time. She went back to her office only to appear at his apartment a few hours later. They picked their way through packing cases, his life still in boxes, since the movers—a company that went by the name We Move U Fast—hadn't turned up to collect. (*You moved me NOT*, William yelled into the phone that morning.) They had sex on a mattress, on the floor. It was raw and hasty, reminding him of student days when everything was improvised and imperative. She made more noise than usual, interesting guttural noises, not at all in keeping with her normal reserve. As he pumped over her, he wondered whether her sounds could be attributed to an anxiety about his leaving town—doubtful, since she'd expressed no concern about it whatsoever—or whether she might be coming into her sexual prime, something he had heard about on *Oprah* while taking one of his frequent breaks from starting his first novel. After, she wanted a drink, so they raided the gift basket that had arrived from her office that afternoon, all that was left in the kitchen: a paltry assortment of pickles and processed cheese, a bottle of champagne, and an envelope.

He inspected the bottle. It was third-rate, practically *méthode Champenoise*. Maybe his new publishing company didn't rate him as highly as he'd hoped. A sobering thought.

William had left Little Co., a one-man show run by the eponymous Robert Little, in favor of the larger Paper House, where Vivian worked as senior editor. His agent, Bart Hopper, had engineered the move: "Little Co. is small beer. You want to know how small? *They didn't ask for an option on your next book.*" William capitulated, not without due damage to his conscience. Little Co. had done well by him. They had published his first book with an unpromising subject: plague-ridden twelfth-century French people. The book had surpassed everyone's expectations and crept its way to the bottom of several best-seller lists. At the time William understood that leaving Little Co. was a Faustian betrayal, made all the more difficult because he liked and admired Robert Little. In the end he'd allowed himself to be agented into the decision with the self-justifying logic that he would need all the help he could get for his next book. Vivian Newman's reputation as an editor was an impetus. So was the fact that Paper House was known for its superior muscle, its strong-arm PR and distribution, and its capacity for large advances.

William turned his attention to the envelope, sandwiched between the Laughing Cow cheese and the sweet-and-sour cucumber: it was remiss of him not to have bothered with it when it arrived. He remembered his mother's words on the etiquette of opening presents, "Always the note first, even if you don't give a shit about what's written inside." His mother was from an upstanding Charleston family. She took perverse pleasure in saying that the respectability of the line had been broken the day she was born. Even so, sometimes her old Southern manners came back to her—when they did, it felt like a supernatural visitation.

Inside the envelope, Vivian's elegant scribble.

Good luck in Los Angeles, from your friends at Paper House.

"You don't realize you're popular until you're leaving," he said. He couldn't help it if it came out a little dry.

"It's not for going," Vivian corrected. "You get a basket on signing and a basket on receipt of an acceptable manuscript."

William thought he heard an ominous emphasis on *acceptable.* That was typical Vivian: clear-eyed, unsparing—probably a little sadistic. Still, she looked formidable standing naked in his kitchen.

She gripped William's wrist, checking his watch for the time. After declaring that they were late—they would have to skip the drink—she left to find her clothes where they'd been dropped in the hall.

William followed. He wasn't about to miss the sight of her stepping into her underwear. He wasn't a fit man—walking around the city and sporadic sex was about the extent of his involvement with the body physical—but to see anatomically correct *gluteus maximus,* twitching and contracting through a range of motion, was to make him believe for a moment it might be worth all that running.

"You're taking all this with you?" Vivian asked, glancing at the boxes stacked high in the hallway. She was tying herself into an ingenious wrap number.

"No. Mostly going into storage—except the books, of course."

He looked around. He'd lost count at thirty of how many boxes of books he felt obliged to transport cross-country. They were his security, proof of sorts that, if nothing else, he was a reader, and that had to count for something.

"The guys that did the packing yesterday," he teased. "They

were your type—iron men with more muscles than probably legal. They were looking at me thinking, If you hadn't wasted your time with so many books, you'd be man enough to do your own packing."

Vivian was in no mood for banter. "They weren't thinking about you at all," she clipped. "More likely composing a paper for night class, or a recipe for bouillabaisse."

William smiled, though he knew he was being cut down. His crime, attempting to be light when the reality was more ambiguous. It was possible that Vivian was feeling the same confounding mixture of regret and relief as he, knowing that whatever they had going was about to end. They would meet again shortly—in less than fifteen minutes to be precise—but everything was about to change between them. With the apartment dismantled and packed, and his own removal the next day, it was understood that his departure would provide a natural break in the relationship, create a physical boundary they had been unable to maintain during their encounters of late. It was a line he'd resolved not to cross as recently as the cab ride to the restaurant, when he'd told himself it wasn't a good idea to let another lunch roll opportunistically into a session at his apartment, even if it was with the mutual understanding that it was for the last time. His intention lasted only from the time he'd paid the fare, to the time he saw her across the table, restlessly crossing and uncrossing her sinewy runner's legs, saw her sweeping jaw, made lovely by her flawless skin, and that determined mouth of hers, relax slightly when she first glanced up, then tense again in readiness to challenge everything he was going to say. His resolution was quickly forgotten, even though common sense had told him that it was in no one's interest to introduce sex into a professional relationship, especially when it involved someone who was married to his oldest friend.

Now that she was dressed, William's amour propre told him it was time to say something that approximated a goodbye. Nothing dramatic, just a simple acknowledgment that there was about to be a shift in their circumstances.

"I'll call you when I get there. I mean, LA, not the restaurant," he said, failing to make any point at all. Vivian's coolness made him all the less so—he didn't even want to begin to consider why that might be the case. Vivian didn't seem to hear. She was preoccupied, checking herself in the mirror. (In stilettos she looked truly Amazonian.) Halfway out the door, she stopped and said, "I'm sure you'll call me when you have a draft." Then she left, heels clicking down the hall.

William ambled along University Place, taking in familiar sights. Each one triggered a series of references, already in the process of being filtered through gauzy mists of nostalgia. It was only natural that some should be pulled into sharper focus, enhanced with an intensity that they didn't have at the time, while others should be left in the fog of the deep background, fading with the possibility that they might be called forward at some later date. That was the beauty of them. They were his for the editing and his only. It was also true that whatever his choices, the imprint of experience would remain an indelible master. For better or for worse, ten years of living in New York had helped make him what he was today.

There was Sal's diner, where Mel served stewed black coffee. William sometimes went there to work: to eat and delete while Mel, seasoned as the huevos rancheros she served, fussed over him with wide-open pride at having a real-life writer typing away at her very own station. There was Mani's newsstand, a twenty-four-hour shrine to the black, white, and glossy. William occasionally stopped there to waste a little time, skim the pages of the tabloids and feel a surge of moral superiority at the lurid tales therein. Then there was the Kim Song Market, where he'd stop on the way back from dinner and marvel at the numbers of late-night shoppers buying milk and waxed fruit. He'd had many an existential moment standing in line there, looking at his fellow travelers, wondering *Who are these people? How did they get here?*

None so existential as the morning five years ago, when he'd gone in to buy milk.

He was reaching inside the cooler at the back of the store, when he'd heard the first plane.

It was too loud. No question something was wrong.

Then, an explosion.

A cry—someone sobbing outside.

A woman: *Oh God, oh God.*

The group—a man, two women, and William—ran outside. Mr. Song left the till hanging open and darted ahead, knocking a giant bottle of ginseng from the counter. The bottle shattered in William's path, forcing him to jump sideways to avoid the naked root, stranded in a pool of glass and amber liquid with its tubers reaching up to him.

They all stood in the street, staring at the smoke billowing on the skyline.

Someone said it was a bomb, a nuclear attack.

No, the smoke's all wrong for that.

It was surreal to hear himself make pronouncements as if he was a member of the Manhattan Project; words, *bomb* and *attack*, when moments before he'd been pondering the difference between the 1 percent and the 2 percent milk. Alarming enough to make him fast-walk two blocks home to his apartment.

As he went, he saw people flowing from cars and buildings, standing in the street with their heads tilted to the sky. He could feel a pull to go with them, yet he needed to resist it. He wanted

to be alone, in a building, away from all the confusion and specu-
lation. He wanted to call someone. His friend Ian Newby came to
mind. Ian was a journalist who had contacts all over town. It was
possible Ian might know something.

Back at his apartment, he couldn't get a line, so he turned on
the television instead.

He watched the news of the second plane on TV, straining his
already tenuous credulity. He had what he believed was a healthy
distrust of television. TV was where fiction happened. If you could
watch King Kong scaling the Empire State Building, you could
watch a model plane going into a digitally altered Twin Tower.
He watched the jumpers jumping. From a distant lens, it seemed
that they went too willingly and fell with a speed that was almost
cartoonish. Like watching Scooby-Doo gallop off a cliff, scramble
in the air, then plummet very fast. *Splat!*

Life couldn't possibly end that way.

On television.

It was a sight that took a while to process.

After the North Tower collapsed, he remembered Esther, who
was eighty-six and lived across the hall.

William had known Esther ten years, since the day he moved
into the building and they'd exchanged shy glances inside the
elevator. When they'd met again outside their apartments—
fumbling keys, more shy looks—William had made a pleasantry,
something about the nice cooking aromas wafting out from under
her door. Esther had peered at him from under drooping folds of
skin. She looked suspicious and slightly aggrieved. Something must
have shifted. She muttered something in Yiddish, made clicking
sounds with her tongue and invited William in to sample the origin
of the smell: *"What you have sensed is but a shadow of the true pleasure."*

At the time William was amused by the voluptuousness of her
promise.

William soon became a frequent visitor to Esther's kitchen. Her glee at having someone eat her *schmaltz* and *flajke* was all the justification he needed to eat onions fried in chicken fat and tripe soup, flagrantly greasy, heart-attack cuisine.

Esther lived quite alone, apart from the attentions of Jujo, a boisterous Jamaican who came to clean once a week, and Rosa, her friend and conduit to the supermarket. She had left Poland after the war. Her family was dead. Her home had been desecrated long before. She had made it to New York with her life and some furniture she'd purchased in 1949 from a shop on Piotrkowska Street, with money her father had placed in the safekeeping of a gentile friend. Whenever William went to Esther's, he left with a feeling that a necromancy had taken place. To step through her door was to be transported to another world, the dying world of an Eastern European émigré. He had the sense that Esther had recreated something of her lost home in her apartment, yet the part that mattered was gone: its absence could be felt as much as what was actually there. He spent many hours there, sifting through books and music, perusing her collection of oil sketches, tantalizingly unsigned. They didn't speak much. She'd already warned him against "too much talk"—she'd made it clear she preferred late Beethoven to conversation. Yet she seemed to appreciate his company, whether it was just to sit watching him eat, or listen with him to Artur Schnabel play the "Hammerklavier" Sonata. Yet, sometimes, apropos of nothing, she did talk, and then she'd come out with details of her internment in the Lodz ghetto. The day her mother had tried to avoid transportation to the death chambers of Chelmno by offering her skeletal body for favor. The day *hell came to earth*: the great liquidation of 1944, of which she had been one of the few to survive. William always listened, rapt. Afterward he'd write notes on what he'd heard. Always the beginning of the horror, never the end. Try as he might, he never could get Esther to say more. Whenever she sensed she was being pushed, she would stop.

That day Esther answered quickly. Either she had galloped across her apartment on her walker or she had been waiting by the door.

He hadn't needed to ask whether she'd seen the news. Her eyes told him the answer. They were stone portals of doom.

"I cannot find Rosa," she'd said.

William knew that Rosa lived and worked in Queens. She was in all likelihood fine.

"I'm sure she's safe. She's probably more concerned about you."

For want of something better to do, he'd asked, "Is there anything you need? Do you want me to pick up some shopping for you?"

But she said, "Come, William. Come sit with me."

It was a simple suggestion, but sitting down had never sounded so great—especially if there was cherry brandy involved. William knew she had some. He suddenly visualized it on the lace-covered cabinet, in her living room. Minutes later, he was sitting on the couch with her, drinking cherry brandy in small, deliberate sips. It was as if he were taking medicine; a palliative against the images of destruction they watched play out on her television screen. Esther held his hand, patting it every so often with her powdery, soft-boned palm. She was grave but unemotional. She kept nodding. Nodding in recognition of the tragedy or out of deference to those who had suffered, William couldn't tell. At one point, her patting seemed to accelerate. William looked down and saw his hand was shaking and Esther's liver-spotted hand was trying to still it. He knew that was the moment the disbelief had worn off.

What followed was an attempt to approximate daily life. William's writing classes at the University began in shell-shocked silence, only to stammer along through the rest of the semester: world events had stunned any impulse to fictionalize them. His classes turned into therapy sessions in which he encouraged his students to explore everything they were seeing and hearing. He had them write accounts of the morning of the eleventh because that's all they could do. The work they produced was impressive. William was struck by how deeply these youngsters empathized with the disaster—more than he could say for himself. William had discovered there was a cutoff point for all that feeling. There was only so much he could take, month after month. Although he would never say it, he was sick of September 11. If the reactionary political climate didn't sicken, the toxic emanations from Ground Zero, the air that smelled of combustion, chemical, electrical, and human, certainly did. He wanted to forget the loss and the suffering that had made that smell.

And stop talking about it.

The days when you could discuss something as pleasurable as a play or a movie had become remote, innocent as pre-puberty, when he'd ride with his father in his car and have golf conversations about the driving power of different clubs. The only time his father engaged with him, and they almost seemed to connect.

A long time ago.

The final indignity was that he was required to think and behave like a fearful person—when he was one already. Before, he could believe he was merely sensitive, with a realist's radar for danger. Now, having to scan every face for a possible terrorist on the subway, or be treated like one every time the paddle of a metal detector passed across his body, was enough to bring out the terror within. As much as he tried to resist the alarmist bulletins, the color-coded security alerts, the Department of Homeland Security had finally won: he was officially scared shitless. William longed for the period of numbness that began the morning of the eleventh, and was over by noon.

William could identify with his students' difficulties in writing. Even before the disaster, he'd been struggling with the beginning chapter of his first novel, about a middle-aged guy who has a breakdown and leaves his family and comfortable life as an academic to become a janitor.

Boring, boring, boring.

After September 11, he had stopped trying to write. It wasn't that big a deal. The novel hadn't been commissioned and the world was in turmoil. For a while it seemed possible that the planes were the first in a fleet, come to take down the rest of the city and reduce it to white ashes. Like his students, the only subjects that interested William were real, not imagined. But only if the events took place over a hundred years ago. Wading though the mire of contemporary politics held no interest for him: which was why eight months later he left for Languedoc to research a work of historical nonfiction, *Days of Plague.*

The book that Robert Little had been good enough to publish.

Without that book, there would have been no move to California. He wouldn't be standing outside the Kim Song Market, late for dinner on the eve of his departure. He was old enough to think in eras—this was definitely the end of the New York period. He could see how it all related.

The eve of what?

He didn't know, and the uncertainty was thrilling.

By the time William arrived, the others had been seated. They were at Gino's, their local trattoria. They went there often, tolerating indifferent food in order to get the treatment: an effusive welcome and the table in the corner. Gino was a stocky third-generation New Yorker. At some point during the meal, he could be counted upon to brandish a large pepper mill and massage it over the plates, like a john masturbating a dildo.

Bob jumped up to shake William's hand and sat down again. Bob was one of life's unshakable enthusiasts. He applied the same energy, always his all, to every task regardless of size, whether he was seasoning the perfect steak or writing an article on the deficit. William and Bob had been history majors together at Princeton, where Bob's bluff amiability and large rented houses had made him the person everyone wanted to know. Through Bob, William had met Ian, and later, Vivian. That was in the days she made coffee and took phone messages for the editor she later replaced.

William leaned down and kissed Vivian's cheek. As he did, he tried to banish images from the afternoon (*what was it about black underwear?*) and concentrate instead on her particular fragrance. It was clean and fresh—something like cucumber. Yes, it was cucumber he'd been smelling all that time.

Ian bared horsey teeth, yellowed from a journalist's diet of cigarettes and coffee. "We thought you'd pissed off already." Ian hadn't lost his English accent in twenty years of working in the States.

This prompted a stream of LA-bashing: the instability of the tectonic plates and inevitability of an earthquake, "a big, cataclysmic mother"; the frozen face of Botox; the obscene sums of money involved in a pre–Academy Award marketing campaign, unkindly referred to as "the price of an Oscar." William listened, smiling only to indulge them. He'd been offered three classes a week at UCLA. That meant time to write. Time they would never have, which was why they were all so bitter.

Bob, like Ian, was a journalist. Bob claimed that during his early days as a reporter he'd been sent to LA to write about the crematoriums. "I broke the story that breast implants were exploding in their hosts. EXPLODING BELOVEDS. You can see the headlines."

"He's making this up," Vivian said for the record.

ETHER

Ian snorted with approval. "Sticky ashes—not nice sprinkly ones you can scatter. You're showing your age, matey. Implants are now biodegradable."

Bob beamed. At thirty-five, he had lost most of his hair. He had one of those faces that refused to change, perpetually cherubic with a shine from overproductive sweat glands. He continued. "I have no problem with California. Blue state, most populous, yet one of our greenest. Our best recyclers are in California. That sadly includes its writers." He stopped, briefly pausing for emphasis. "As for LA. You have to love it. The boomtown mentality— everyone on the make. It seduces you, the decadent ease of living. You give your car keys to a total stranger every time you move your car, but you have to wonder if Angelenos haven't got it right. Where's the merit in our daily struggle to park? Are we better people for spending our lives circling the block, cursing our fellow beings? I've always had a fantasy that I'd live and die in LA."

"Suffocated between two mounds of silicone, no doubt," Vivian said dryly.

"A logical conclusion," Ian agreed.

Bob slipped his arms around Vivian's waist. William saw he stopped short of squeezing her tiny breast. "Nonsense—I'll only die beside you. My beautiful wife."

William saw she didn't pull away from him.

He had been observing them in awe. It was an inescapable fact that Bob and Vivian were good together. While William had slept with Vivian, maybe, five times in nine months, they had stayed married for twenty years. Their solidarity was formidable. It made William realize his insignificance, that he had never penetrated their relationship—not that he'd tried or even wanted to.

The conversation moved on to the president's military junta and the prisoners in Guantánamo Bay. The rise of Bible-Belt fundamentalism.

"You realize we are the scourge, the new minority?" Ian said, toasting himself.

Afterward, on the pavement, among expressions of bonhomie, he'd fallen to his knees, imploring, "Take me with you. I'll be your factotum-slash-roommate. Von Stroheim to your Swanson."

William had to offer his arm, seeing Ian was having difficulty getting up. It was a sad fact of life they were both too old for horseplay.

Then it was time to leave.

Bob, always a hugger, gave William a bear of one.

Ian slapped him on the back.

Vivian mustered a perfunctory kiss—all William would have expected in the proximity of her husband.

But when she leaned into him, William felt her nails digging into his arm.

Hard.

William was startled. It was unlike her to make any kind of gesture, albeit a passive-aggressive one. If they'd been alone, he might have made a joke about her needing a manicure. Since they weren't, he let the moment pass.

Time to go.

He walked away, leaving them on the pavement to talk about him, he knew, and predict shattered dreams—the prevailing wisdom about writers who went to Hollywood. He was glad to be leaving, just in case things were about to get messy with Vivian. Even so, there was a serious possibility he might miss them all.

The terminal doors parted and the air hit him, warm and sweet. William stood for a moment, taking in the crowd of meeters and greeters. Some idled in vehicles, defying a voice that intoned a warning about parking on the white line, while others passed time on cell phones or walked restless children. Only the most persistent had made it inside, clumped with messages of welcome and balloons. He wondered what these people could hope for: the embrace of a loved one, or a cursory nod and a dumped suitcase? It occurred to him that an airport was where expectation and reality failed to meet. That accounted for heightened emotions—or the lack of them.

At the barrier he'd passed an elderly couple clutching a gas-station bouquet: tired roses and a frizz of baby's breath, and his thoughts were drawn back to Esther. He'd managed to avoid all thought of her on the plane by slumping into an unconscious sleep, thanks to a cocktail of Bloody Mary and altitude, mixed in with fatigue. The previous night, the combination of mover's anxiety, the Esther situation, and a telephone message left on his answering machine when he was in the shower, was a sure recipe for insomnia. Vivian's low voice: "I'm sorry if I was tense tonight. Things are more complicated than you realize. No need to respond. Please, no condolences. Remember, I'm not expecting to hear from you until due day." He hadn't speculated on what those complications might be—he could probably figure out the broad strokes—what concerned him was that the way she said *due day* was definitely loaded.

The fact was, he'd left Esther in a dire state: arguably one for which he was partly responsible. The problems had started the moment he'd told her he was leaving. He'd delayed telling her until ten days before, calculating that it was enough time for her to adjust to the idea but not so much to allow her to dwell on it. He realized that his leaving would be a loss of vital companionship and a blow to her well-being. The chances of the next tenant taking an interest in an ailing octogenarian had to be on the low side of low. Whatever he'd supposed, he hadn't anticipated how badly she'd take the news.

Her eyelids had fluttered—unusual for someone who never seemed to blink—then her eyes rolled back. When she wouldn't respond to his entreaties, William thought she was having a stroke.

An ambulance arrived: screaming sirens and a gurney.

"How are you feeling, ma'am?" a medic said, examining an undilated pupil.

"He knows," she said, glancing at William so there would be no mistaking the source of her ills.

As her vital signs were fine, the medics left, unimpressed by the urgency of the situation.

But stubbornly, as if to prove a point, she got worse.

She stopped talking. She stopped moving, seemingly resigned to sit in her own wastes. Instead of cabbage and *kreplach*, her apartment now stank of urine. A disturbing smell. Not so much because of the actual odor—he was familiar enough with the stink of piss—but because of what it represented: deterioration, incapacitation, old age, and all its indignities.

William had never witnessed this kind of physical decline. He hadn't known any of his grandparents. His mother, Delia Chatton, had seen to that. Always one to divide and conquer, Delia had skillfully kept both sets, paternal and maternal, at bay. She had applied the same principle to her own parenting, with the mixed result that not only had she separated William from his father, but William was also cued to stay the hell away from her as well. When it had come to his parents' retirement years, his father organized his affairs well in advance with a double-booking at the Rainbow Assisted Living Home in Palm Bay, Florida. When the time came, William was presented with a hair-combed, diaper-changed, wheeled-in-wheeled-out, sanitized version of life before death. An additional convenience for his father was that Alzheimer's had given flight to his wife's caprices and personality disorders, leaving in their place a mild-mannered and compliant old sweetie. While William was glad to see his father settled and content, with his wife under control after the long turbulence of their marriage, his mother's alteration was far less comfortable. For all the years he'd spent trying to shrug off her instability and dramatic ways, there was familiarity there, and the idea, however illusory, that one day they would enter a calm, adult phase together—a hope he hadn't even realized he had been nursing until it was gone. To see the vacant shell of Delia Chatton in "circle time," shiny-eyed and holding hands with her husband on the one side, and some senile sister on the other, was to acknowledge what could never be: that a landscape without his mother as he knew her was a far less rich and interesting place than it had been before.

With Esther, William found himself in an impossible situation. While he wasn't going to pass up an opportunity and stay on with her, he was now starting to feel like a heartless shit for not doing so. It was as if he had taken on the burden of an aging parent and was suddenly being made to feel all the weight of obligation it implied.

When he'd raised his concerns on the phone to Rosa, he had met with irritable response. Rosa, herself a harried mother of four, had inherited the responsibility of Esther from her own mother, now deceased.

"What do you want me to say? I think she's eighty-six. You're looking for permission to leave? You've got it."

"I don't see how Esther can sustain herself."

"Got any better ideas?" Rosa asked.

"No. I'm all out of ideas today," he'd replied with a little more attitude than was probably necessary. "I don't even know what she lives on."

"Unless you're thinking of getting involved, it's really none of your business," Rosa said before ringing off.

As galling her manner, he knew that Rosa was right: he needed to commit to Esther or leave. When he thought about it, he had to admire the chutzpah of this small bird, who weighed less than eighty pounds, for trying to control what he did with his life. She wasn't family. Or was she? Things became a little murky when he asked himself that question. In a cynical moment, he'd wondered what she had done to deserve his loyalty, apart from plying him with fatty, death-invoking foods. Yet he realized the question was redundant, designed to steer him away from what he knew. The answer was embedded in the memory of her powder-soft hand, the solace of her touch. How different from Vivian's cold nails the day before. When Vivian said, *Please, no condolences*, he knew she wanted him to call. To get into some convoluted discussion about their relationship and the state of her marriage—one to avoid. In the end, he decided that what he was going through with Esther was no different from any child who, torn between two paths, chose the one that favored its own interest over that of the parent. It happened every day.

Well, it did in his own family anyway.

W illiam navigated the grid fairly easily. La Cienega to Sunset. Left on Hillgard. At the rental place, he'd thrown over a virtuous Prius in favor of a Mustang convertible. A commitment that lasted only the distance of the lot, when the roof failed to retract, leaving him half-mast and feeling less like Jimmy Dean than the old captain of a sailing junk. Sitting on a plastic chair, surrounded by gleaming vehicles—*an impressive selection: you'd never get that at LaGuardia*—he waited for his original choice to be prepared. He even enjoyed a few minutes of sun. The irony that he had traveled three and a half thousand miles to sunbathe in a parking lot wasn't lost on him. For a moment's folly, justice had been served.

The weather had made him do it: an irresistible combination of heat and breeze, a sultry balm that would be forever associated with school holidays in Miami. They weren't official breaks, but ones force majeured by his mother in the middle of the term, which made them all the more vivid, all the more of a reprieve. She would arrive at his prep school in the freeze of a New England December and announce in her most kittenish manner (it was embarrassing), *I have to take my son*—no explanation was apparently ever given or required. They'd make their escape, flying south like swallows. For the duration of the first two flights, she'd talk nonstop on free-ranging subjects: her housekeeper's private life, her latest couture purchases, complaints that her precious butterfly garden was going to seed because of pecuniary restrictions imposed by that *monster*, his father. By the third plane, she would be out cold, a combination of alcohol and white pills, only to revive again during the journey's final segment, the cab ride to the beach, reanimated by the sunlight and bleached colors, the faded kitsch she adored. They'd check into the nicest hotel on South Beach, in the days when a nice hotel on South Beach was a rarity, and drink outsize concoctions by the pool, while his mother overflowed with praise for his cleverness and poise, quickly contrasted with his father's boorishness. By the end of her tirade, she would have snapped all the cocktail umbrellas into pieces, and the waiter, seeing William's dismay, would bring him more to take up to the room. William knew that when his father found out about their tryst he would be affronted to the core. He already saw her particular brand of uncontrolled whimsy as subversive—to be opposed at all costs. William sometimes felt sorry for him: a man who'd spent his entire life at Steers and Chatton, upholding the banners of conservatism and trust law; a man whose hair had turned white before it dropped out at thirty, apparently from the sheer boredom of it all.

William quickly learned the best way of handling her was to keep quiet and pretend to listen, freeing his attention for his own pursuits, his own observation for one. Poolside rituals were always good for a while: couples greasing up, different shades of toast, a man's large form lurking below the water's surface like a hippopotamus, a woman licking a drip of ice cream from an inner thigh and her *enormous* breasts—he'd coined the term *melonious* specially for them. What followed then was an unsteady meander back to the room, where she'd sprawl on the bed and fall asleep. He'd drape her with a blanket, not as an act of consideration, but as a protective measure against the sinister dark hairs creeping out from the edges of her bathing suit. He'd watched copious amounts of television, most of it adult, and it had given him a complicated relationship with pornography ever since.

At first sight La Cienega was unremarkable, a string of fast-food stores, gas stations, and discount shops. But as the road climbed up past the oil wells—rusted cranes slowly pecking the ground—he began to notice the geophysical presence of the land. It dipped and rolled with a sculptural majesty. The suburban outcrops had the look of an unsuccessful art gallery installation; an awkward imposition that in spite of itself had an integrity, an insistence that it be called *Art*. As he drove, he had a sense of space expanded—the infamous and sultry LA sprawl. He experienced it as a release, much as you would the loosening of tight seams. He understood what the settlers must have felt to go so far west you can't go any farther.

A sense of arrival.

Finally, the road sloped down and passed through more prosperous neighborhoods, with cafés and restaurants and a smarter mall or two. It rose up again one last time, before stopping at the foot of the Hollywood Hills. There they were—an eclectic scattering of homes on this hillside: Mediterranean villa by tract house, rancher's cabin next to adobe palace—far more desirable than he had been led to believe. He would like to have stopped but the traffic swept him along. Turning left, he continued, hugging the curves of the roads.

There's something sexy about driving on Sunset.

The apartment was clean and functional; no more and no less than William would have expected from a place chosen off the Web for its proximity to the campus. After hoisting the blinds, the porter pointed out views of the main drag: the Starbucks, the generic combo of offices, retail, and residential. He indicated the general direction of the university, only ten minutes' walk away, depending on your pace. Here he looked at William, doubtful. More interesting to William was the sight of the freeway shortcutting behind that was beginning to look more and more like an escape route to somewhere. He made a note to himself to find out where.

William could see that his chosen location of Westwood, an area developed in the seventies—or as Ian would have it, a postmodern village conceived by Mickey Mouse—was designed for people like himself: a purpose-built transit lounge for those in search of a new life. He gave himself the length of his rental agreement: six months to a year max.

The porter made an energetic show of the shower, microwave, cabinets, and drawers, and left, not before offering William *whatever* he needed. Judging by his jumped-up enthusiasm, William took that to mean speed or sex, or possibly both.

Now that he was alone, he went back to the window. He watched people on the street moving silently around. All sound was sealed, double-glazed tight. To an ear attuned to the hum and shout of the city, the silence was disconcerting. It made him feel weightless. A fish in a bowl, bobbing agog at the world outside.

He checked the telephone to make sure it was connected.

No one knows I'm here. I could die before anyone would notice.

He imagined what it would be like to arrive in a city and, literally, not know anyone. A soul-destroying loneliness. The thought of it made him uneasy—an indulgence when he really did have people to call. There was Red Stevens, the Aussie production designer. There was the department, to say he'd arrived. He had one or two other numbers, belonging to friends of friends, but he had taken them only out of politeness, in the hope he wouldn't need them.

His money was on Red Stevens. Red was a hoot. Red would take care of him—or so he hoped.

He dialed the number and was relieved when Red answered and let out a roar of recognition. "You coming to a party tonight, mate?" William was glad he still said *mate.*

He had met Red in the bar at an opening at the Met. Red had impressed him with his knowledge of Renaissance pigments. Red designed big period movies and had recently reconstructed parts of eighteenth-century Manhattan in a studio near Queens. They met again over a period of six months: at an art opening, at dinner—William even ran into him in Central Park, where Red confessed to be out *trawling.* William always enjoyed Red's company. His capacity for laughter: loud. His sensibility: surprisingly refined. His energy: sexually omnivorous. At their most recent encounter, a dinner at the home of a Park Avenue philanthropist, William noted that no matter how erudite the company, no matter how many PhD's there were at the table, the conversation would always steer back to Red's experiences in Hollywood. Red would be coaxed to tell stories about a difficult actress or a megalomaniac director. As much disdain as there was for the movie business, there was fascination in equal parts. Anecdotes about the barbarians out west were greeted with a mixture of schadenfreude and envy, but for the civilized New Yorker, they were ultimately life-affirming.

Red's place was downtown. He'd told William that no sane person lived downtown. By the looks of things, he was right. He lived in a row of industrial warehouses and derelict parking lots. The only sign of life: a row of expectant valets waiting on the curb. William pulled up beside them, conscious of the fact he was casually dropping his keys into the willing hands of a stranger.

Inside Red's loft, he was assaulted by sounds: a kind of New Age techno-rap and maybe a hundred bodies, crammed into the space. He couldn't help wondering about their cars. Where were they? They must have been hidden away, presumably for effect: wasteland cut to chic, modernist loft. He squeezed through a group of young women sporting cropped tanks and pierced bellies. They were drinking out of plastic cups and swaying to the music. It scared him that they were probably still in their teens. And there were boys, so many good-looking boys. In an instant, William felt old.

"Author, author," someone shouted.

He felt some meaty fists grab him from behind, then humidity, as a sweating body pressed into him.

He turned around to see Red beaming from a blaze of manic hair. On the basis of hair color alone, he should have been called Orange. William remembered why he had liked Red on sight. This unlikely aesthete looked and drank like a lumberjack, not a tasteful fabricator of interiors.

With a powerful grip, he dragged William across the room.

"Come meet Madeline. The star of my last movie."

William protested, "Please. Allow me to recover from the shock of the beautiful people—"

But Red wouldn't hear of it. "Bollocks. You're meeting her now. She's smart and gorgeous, and she's even read your bloody book."

Even with the large sales of his book, it still took William by surprise to hear of a putative reader. He was trying to calculate whether it was more meaningful to discover a book independently, or be given it by a friend, when he saw a young woman across the room.

She was in the corner, talking to someone. It had to be her. They were heading in her direction. She looked vaguely familiar, and she was the only woman in the room to whom a superlative could apply. William had seen enough pretty girls in his time. He'd even known a few. Manhattan was full of them. They could be seen laughing in restaurants or rushing in and out of cabs. What they had in common was a uniformity of features: the blank canvas kind that could be transformed by makeup and lighting. Rarely did they have presence.

Madeline was the exception.

Hers was a face you might see on a wall in the Uffizi or a hall in the Louvre: unadorned, serious loveliness.

"And she's a nice person. She's into civil rights and whatnot," Red said, depositing him, a reluctant load, in front of her. "Be nice to William—he's straight off the banana boat." Then Red left William with Madeline and a friend who was glaring at him, unhappy about being interrupted. The friend soon ceded her territory and went elsewhere.

Her eyes: fractured quartz.

She said, "I read your book."

She paused long enough for him to say, "Not exactly light entertainment."

"I read it on a stopover to Darfur."

Stopover to Darfur—an ironic title for something?

"You couldn't find anything better in the 'Apocalypse' section?"

She had a modest smile. Not too broad or toothy.

She sipped her drink through a straw on the side of her mouth, explaining that she'd gone to the Sudan with a friend associated with a humanitarian organization, trying tragically after the fact to raise awareness of a genocide. No surprise they'd found it difficult getting public attention and financial support.

"You know how it is—when there isn't a vested interest . . ."

Her cheeks turned a high color. That was endearing. William didn't think anyone blushed anymore.

When at last she said, "I loved your book. It really affected me," he could finally relax and be modest.

"It was meant to disappear quietly but it got out of hand."

"That's because we all can totally relate. Nothing has changed. War, disease, persecution—it's the same today. And yet life went on, people took their chances, fell in love, had children. That's comforting."

Her vehemence was surprising. "It is?"

"Yeah, it makes me believe that whatever goes on is part of a cycle, a continuing—stop me, if I sound spiritual . . ."

He felt like saying, *No, you sound like someone I could love.*

"And what about Georges and Thérèse? You made that up, right? Or at least embellished?"

"No, it was in the church records. The pastor was a gifted writer. I merely transcribed and translated—did a little scene-setting. I was incredibly fortunate to find that story."

Here he wasn't being modest. He knew how lucky he'd been to find an untapped source in a field plowed by historians with more experience than himself. All the more so, when he considered how tenuous his original connection with the material had been—he'd stumbled upon it after a teenage road trip had gone south. After getting his baccalaureate, he'd left Massachusetts in the company of a luscious classmate, Marie de Castignac. The idea was for them to travel around the Pyrenees in the steps of the French historian Ladurie, whose *Montaillou* was an iconic book of scholarship. After their expedition, generously financed by her father, they were to head over to her family château outside Nice for some recreation of a more gymnastic sort. The plan was aborted after a row outside Paris ended with Marie abandoning their car shrieking, *Go to hell, leetle man. Imbecile. Preek!* forcing William to complete the pilgrimage, now a point of honor, alone. By chance he stopped at the tiny village of Mas-le-Dur, etched in the mountain of Le Dur. Mas dated from the eleventh century and was little-known outside the region, probably as it was overshadowed by its more celebrated neighbor. There, in the church, he saw a funeral relief: the figures of a man and woman lying side by side. They were facing each other. Instead of the usual devotional and pious stares, there was something earthbound, distinctly secular about their gaze.

William was intrigued by the inscription. Roughly translated, it read:

In the cold and heavy stone,
a song of bliss, and lover's love
yield a small stirring
in a reader's heart,
and death once more will be denied
Georges Le Gorce

That's what happened. Eight hundred years after those words were written, a small stirring took place: William was moved and a notion implanted that he should find out more about the author, Georges Le Gorce. It took William another fifteen years to act on the idea and return, inspired by a desire to write something historical that was in some way literary.

His first success came in tracking down the last surviving descendant of Monsieur Péri, priest of the church at Mas, one Madame Magnier, who was living in shabby isolation in the remains of a fifteenth-century farm near Montségur with a few dozen sheep. His second success was in charming her with his fluent, perfectly accented conversation. (Here he could finally absolve his mother for pulling him from his father's alma mater and dropping him into the lycée speaking no French, a cruel and unusual punishment at the time.) William was granted access to her papers, stored in vaults beneath the house, alongside some interesting-looking vintages. There he found a trove in the form of a diary written by Péri, a substantial source that brought both Chaucer and Pepys to mind. Péri told tales of parish life, a provincial society blighted by plague and poverty and divided by religious conflict. He took special interest in documenting corruption within the church, reserving his most colorful prose for the sodomy he claimed was rampant among the clergy. He was not above paying loving attention to the physical prowess of the noble Georges Le Gorce, a youth of beauty and stamina, who at great personal risk had gone out from the safety of his domain to tend the health of his ailing tenants. According to Péri, his heart was taken by Thérèse Millier, the daughter of a local stonemason. Thérèse became pregnant by Georges and bore him a son before falling victim to contagion herself. Georges nursed Thérèse from near-death back to health, a recovery so remarkable that it spurred rumors that it was unnatural; that she must have made a pact with the devil to save her life in return for another's. After Georges's rapid decline and death, suspicion quickly hardened into accusation. Thérèse was charged with the Albigensian heresy, the recusancy du jour, condemned, and burned. Her son was taken by Church authorities and never seen again. Georges's family did nothing to protect her, denouncing her and her illegitimate child. The fact that Georges's younger brother bore no children and the Le Gorce line died with him was taken as further proof of Thérèse's accursedness and sorcery. The account was handed down to successive generations of Péris who became landlords and sheep farmers and had taken little interest in it. William was first to be granted access to Madame Magnier's forgotten archive, if only because he was the first to have asked. The story of Thérèse and Georges formed the heart of his book. They became William's Juliet and Romeo. His Eloise and Abelard.

"It's romantic. The way he puts himself at risk to nurse her when she's sick," Madeline said.

"And is ravaged by disease," William said, sounding more sadistic than he intended. He could tell she didn't like it.

"Tell me that isn't romantic," she asked, her voice lowering into a register of disappointment. Her question was a challenge. There was clearly a correct answer and an incorrect one.

"It isn't romantic. I mean—it is romantic."

Then someone came over to her. The young woman whom he hadn't even acknowledged—big mistake. She had gone away and had come back to sabotage their conversation. This Romy made it clear that they were going to meet some friends for dinner and he wasn't invited. William kicked himself for not having been nicer to her—that had been a major miscalculation. But then Madeline said goodbye with warmth and sincerity, and William was emboldened to shuffle in his pockets to scribble his phone number on the corner of a ticket stub, which she took, eyes creased with amusement.

What an ass. What was I thinking? Pushing my phone number on her. I blew it.

Back in the apartment, William couldn't sleep. The bed was hard and uninviting. The sheets, stiff and unbroken. He padded back and forth, stopped to look at himself in the bathroom mirror. He needed to see what she had seen, deduce what kind of impression he might have made.

His eyes stared back: deep-set, moccasin, quietly determined, a glint of humor, no, more like irony. The willfulness, he recognized. It bore an unsettling resemblance to his mother's inimitable brand—something he'd never noticed before. He'd seen that look when his father paced around waving a handful of bills, evidence of extravagance, while his mother sat tight, unapologetic as an innocent, until his father gave up and disappeared back into his study.

He considered his teeth. They were a disaster—a mess of overlapping piano keys. He was exaggerating to think that included some of the black notes. First evening at school, he'd tried to flush his retainer down the toilet after hearing an inmate being taunted with the terrifying epithet *girly mouth*, for possession of such a device. When the item was found by a cleaner, his housemaster confronted him and William denied all knowledge of it. Unfortunately for his palate, his mother wasn't available to either confirm or deny the accusation, so his expensive hardware was relegated to lost property along with Latin primers and wayward socks, only to be regretted at that very moment.

He tried alternating his expression: steely judgment melting into compassionate interest, but his brow held its furrow, which made him look bemused. Still, vulnerability wasn't a bad thing. A woman needed a man who could be sensitive, with the exception of Vivian, who he hoped didn't need anything. He was older than he would have liked, a sprinkling of silver told him that, but at least his hair was somewhat plentiful, unlike some people's he knew. He was carrying more weight than he should, but with a sedentary profession he wasn't going to start worrying about that. He had a good strong head. Read: large—full of brains. Would this countenance inspire a beautiful young woman to pick up the telephone and dial a strange, older man?

Countenance plus book?

He felt his confidence drain away. His head, light with fatigue.

He flopped into bed, closing his eyes, but her face seared into his vision and it seemed to be looking at his over-big head and his ridiculous graying hair. He felt sick to his stomach. Why was he suddenly attacking himself? It was so unlike him: a madness, surely. Was this some kind of Hollywood malaise?

He thought about masturbating, but decided against it. He didn't want to dilute the memory of the evening. Usually when he desired a woman he saw himself fucking her, but tonight that wasn't appropriate. His imagination balked at the idea as debasing. You didn't fuck a goddess—you worshipped her with the hope that that also might involve making love in a thousand tantric positions. What he'd felt that night wasn't lust, the urge in the groin that made him want to pick up the phone and call Vivian, but something different: a need to connect.

A profound sense of longing.

On the way to Red's, Madeline had sat on the freeway for ninety minutes without moving. After twenty, she'd snapped off the radio. K-Rock didn't sound so good when sitting stationary. The alternative on NPR was even less appealing: a group of senators justifying the war. She wondered why politicians were so totally inept at their jobs. In any other profession they would be fired immediately.

With four lanes of stalled traffic and news helicopters above, it didn't take her long to figure out there was an accident ahead. With no exit in sight and time for reflection, she could see her declining of Romy's offer to pick her up—she'd wanted to preserve the option of bailing last minute—had been selfish and neurotic. The idea that Romy might be five cars away was as pathetic as it was environmentally unsound.

Sitting in the car without the benefit of distraction, Madeline had time to think about the nagging anxiety that had become part of her day. It was eroding her confidence, making her a bad friend. It was undesirable, totally untenable. She could see how close she was to becoming a weird old recluse. She could see her options were simple: it was time to get help and look for a therapist—either that or she'd better start looking for a good medication.

For a while now she'd had a low-grade phobia, manifest in the dread of social events any bigger than a one-on-one with a friend. It was an effort to get out of the house; to get dressed up, or rather dressed down, because going out in LA meant perfecting a studied casualness. That meant the right jeans, the right T-shirt, makeup, but never too much—unless it was a premiere, then a team would arrive with enough clothes and accessories to fill a small boutique. Her manager, Martha Mondel, hadn't helped by telling her to never go out ungroomed, even to the dog trainer.

You never know who's going to be there, snapping at you with a cell phone. You'll end up in the Enquirer *looking like the missing Olsen triplet.*

When going out served a professional purpose, when there was a clear motivation, she had no problem getting herself together. She didn't know what that meant. Hopefully she could pay someone who could tell her.

One thing for sure, there was a connection between elevated anxiety and the commotion accompanying the release of her last two movies. The films, both high-end thrillers, had gone on to make astronomical amounts at the box office, marking her ascendancy as the brightest new star. Her position in the constellation made her uneasy and showed what professional success could and couldn't do. Sure, it had bought her some freedoms: access to better material, much better pay, free clothes and spa days and all the dinners she could eat, but it also meant she had lost the ability to feel her way forward guided by the promise of something, a fantasy of what life would be like if it were different. Now that she had achieved a version of a dream, she had woken to the stakes and what it meant not to achieve them. From this lofty elevation, she could see how fast the parameters of expectation changed. How quickly just getting by was replaced by bigger ambitions—now that anything less than A-list stardom was no longer an option. At the age of twenty-three, she'd always thought nostalgia was something she might look forward to in a distant, retired future. Yet already she found herself fondly remembering the days when work was more like child's play sustained by small roles, commercials, classes, and auditions. There was something oppressive about this high-powered grown-up's club, with a membership permanently up for renewal. It made her see the reality of a business where careers were controlled by corporate entities, actors evaluated by the sum of their grosses, work determined by casting lists that were short and changeable: what it took to get on the list was a nebulous combination of box-office success, perceived fabulousness, and luck.

Most alarming was the effect her new profile had on people. All the fuss and attention ran against the reasons she'd wanted to become an actor: for the fun of donning a mask and disappearing inside a role; to be anonymous and forget herself, and all the reasons for wanting to escape. Now, even at private parties people stared, did comical double takes, making no effort to conceal their interest, as if she was behind a one-way mirror where she could be viewed and her watchers remain unseen. Strangers treated her like a familiar (always a catch, some favor to be asked) and familiars could be distant, as a shift in her circumstances meant a shift in the ground of their relationship. Even her friend Romy couldn't conceal the rue in her eyes at the sight of such an excess of good fortune. And then there were the fans that had been turning up at her place in increasing numbers. This strange breed, lumbering in anoraks in warm weather, came prepared to stay from the cool of the morning through the midday heat, night through morning again. They appeared with folders of photographs downloaded from the Internet, stills from films she'd rather were forgotten. They made her want to move away from her loft in Venice, where anyone could walk up, to a house with high walls and security cameras. That didn't mean to say that enthusiasm was always unwelcome: in her local market, they had put up flyers for her film, a boy's cries of admiration, weaving past on his bicycle made her smile, and there were the approving clucks from the organic lady as she wrapped chard at the farmers market.

The last years of intense location work meant that what came between had started to feel like a lull between jobs. (That is, excluding minor storms: the clashing opinions of her manager, Martha Mondel, versus her agent, Sue Black. The deluge of scripts and phone calls to discuss them.) It was hard for her to feel present when she was always looking ahead. So when a friend offered her a place on the trip to Sudan, she said yes. She wanted to do something that was bigger than herself.

Darfur was epic: human suffering on a grand scale. Within moments of arriving, she realized that anything less than committing her life to try and help ease the misery was lip service. Ten days and a check would never be enough. Humbled and guilty that she didn't have the stamina to stay, she went as a concerned bystander and left an ashamed tourist because she had no stomach for corrupt government, extreme poverty, and half-dead children. Yet it was a place that altered her. She'd come back wanting to become worthy of her pampered Western privileges. She didn't know exactly how she would do it, but she knew living life as if she was biding time between projects wasn't it.

An ambulance and two fire trucks screamed past in the fire lane, leaving in their wake a shrill reminder of what was going on ahead. Someone maimed—a fatal accident, somebody's child, sister, or mother. Romy—as if she wasn't feeling bad enough. She was able to dismiss the thought, remembering how Romy was always first in, last out of parties. Romy always said that every social occasion was an opportunity from which a benefit could be extracted. Her self-avowed "party lust" meant that she had probably arrived, and was already working the room.

The traffic crept forward. Soon she passed the site of the collision; she'd been closer to it than she'd realized. Littered on the side, a blown-out tire, a cracked side mirror, a ripped-off door. They might have been body parts given all the dread they inspired. The scene already had the look of history: something past and unchangeable that would be subject to debate, different versions of what actually happened. With a shudder she realized that if she had left her apartment a few minutes earlier, it might have been her Lexus hybrid that was without a door or an owner.

The cars in front nudged forward. Soon the traffic began to flow again.

Finally, some acceleration.

She left the scene with an unbottled relief at her escape and wondered whether she was selfish to be so glad when others hadn't been so lucky. She told herself, no. It was important to attach value to every moment. *You give life its meaning—not the other way around.*

High up on the ramp, the sun seemed to be melting into the city. The oncoming traffic had become liquid, white streams of light. After treading water for so long, she felt as though she was riding a wave, and it was carrying her to an interaction that would be meaningful. It was a rare feeling of connectedness that felt like the beginning and end of something. Later, she would look back on that moment and wonder if what she'd felt was hopefulness. A hope that came with wanting something and believing in the possibility of finding it, and wonder whether she had put herself into the mind-set that she needed to fall in love and marry because she didn't want to be alone anymore. To be half of a couple was to be half as scared. Two was greater than one—or so logic told her at the time.

If she hadn't recognized his name, she might not have noticed him. He was short, obviously out of shape, and slightly balding. But the moment he started talking, he became savagely attractive to her. He had a hungry air as if he was hunting for something and might not be too happy if he didn't find it. He had a point of view and learning to back it up.

His feral teeth were sort of interesting.

He was a man, not a boy—that part was important.

He was unlike anyone she had ever met.

Sometime after 2:00 a.m., William had turned off his computer. Overstimulated and unable to rest, he'd given up on the notion of sleep and decided to work instead. He'd managed twenty pages of a new story. Not a bad count, mostly atmosphere, written stream-of-consciousness without his usual painstaking care. He didn't know where it was going, but he felt sure he was onto something: a tale that began with the intersection of two people, *William and Madeline* (names to be changed—useful only as a starting point), an examination of the crazy-making milieu of a young actress, and a culture that prized beauty above health, celebrity beyond everything—with her relationship with her putative lover in there somewhere. Of course he was mining territory he had stepped into the night before. That was of no great concern. His experience in fiction writing, limited to a handful of stories in short form, told him that writing was a discovery, a path that could be revealed only as he progressed. The backbone of the trail, the ideas and characters, could only be found channeled by that mysterious process that took place somewhere between the brain and the page. By the time his characters had run the gauntlet of the journey, they would be battered out of all recognition. Whatever it was, it felt good to be writing again. It had been over a year since *Days of Plague* and he hadn't been able to start anything.

He woke to the sound of the phone ringing.

It took several seconds to remember he was in Westwood not Manhattan, another few to think of the two Madelines, the fictional and real—although they'd barely left him and seemed to have permeated his dreams.

Hearing her voice on the end of the line, it was as if they'd multiplied into three.

"Er, hi. This is Madeline. I'm looking at houses with a Realtor today. I was wondering whether you'd like to come, take an architectural tour of the city. Thought it might be interesting for you."

He'd stumbled. "Yes, that would be . . . how incredibly nice of you to think of me."

"I'd like the company," was her even nicer reply.

Twenty-five minutes later, she was idling outside in her car.

As she drove, William stole peeks at her lovely profile. He liked the way her nose seemed to have been chiseled, with the sculptor adding one extra tap, a tiny articulation at the very end. She sat low, swamped in a capacious seat, head and shoulders barely above the wheel. She reminded him both of a child in a parent's car and a beautiful old lady in her eccentric flopsy sun hat.

She explained that she was house-hunting on her accountant's advice that it was expedient for her to get herself a mortgage. Also, there was the more urgent problem that she was having "privacy issues" with fans. When William saw the scale of the first mansion in Brentwood, he judged her mortgage would be a sizable one and that her earning power had to be equally awesome. As for her privacy issues, he imagined it was nothing that a good security system and a millionaires' community wouldn't fix. It was hard to imagine any teenyboppers marauding up such serene and exclusive hills.

Madeline's Realtor, Bunny Jones, was a woman for all times. With a style that nodded to fifties icons Lucille Ball and Elvis Presley, and a fully scalpeled face courtesy of the post-surgical millennium, she was buyer's coach and cheerleader, friend to the house-hunting super-rich. She was easy and familiar, and quick to quip, but her fast-talking breeze belied the ambition of a woman whose drive kept her in business years after many would have retired, and in skinny pants generations after their invention.

Bunny quickly pegged William as a noncelestial person and took him aside to advertise her vast experience: forty years of selling homes to *all the stars*. She guided William and Madeline through seven bedrooms that had the look of deluxe hotel rooms, an eat-in kitchen with an island large enough to float an entire family, a fifteen-seat screening room, pitching the lifestyle as she went. "After say a little cocktail, an alfresco dinner party—you saw the *divine* patio—you can screen your movies. You'd never need to go out. Right?" The expanses of marble reminded William of mausoleums and his own inevitable death. The absence of anything personal—not one book, brush, or shoe, only paintings done by the yard by an artist who liked his women wrapped in feather boas and little else—compounded his sense of having one foot in the shrine and the other in the tomb. As far as William could tell, the only sign of humanity was the smell of fresh-roasted coffee in the kitchen. A Realtor's trick: bread in the oven and a coffee bean in the microwave was an old professional's ruse to create instant homeyness when there was none.

By gosh, he sniffed, *it kind of works.*

He couldn't tell what Madeline was thinking. She walked around opening doors and cupboards with the deadpan expression of a professional surveyor. William sincerely hoped she didn't approve. He had to tell himself not to get ahead—to stop thinking proprietarily about their future home.

When they were back in the privacy of her car, she laughed and said, "If I lived there, I'd kill myself—use the marble for a headstone. My epitaph could be *She recycled to the end*."

Her reaction pleased him. He thought that boded well.

On their way to another exclusive enclave twenty-five minutes away (he was discovering that everything in LA was twenty-five minutes away), William coaxed Madeline to talk a little about herself.

Her mother lived in West Covina, a destination famed for its car dealerships.

She had a divorced sister, Shona, who had two girls whom she rarely saw.

Her father was an artist. He'd separated from her mother just after she'd left high school and drunk himself to death. This was told in the matter-of-fact tones of an experienced Al-Anon participant.

She was rueful when she said that she hadn't been to college, but had moved to New York to pursue an acting career instead.

She was leaving in a week to start a film in North Carolina.

Hearing this, William was seized by a sense of urgency. Whatever was going to happen needed to happen fast, otherwise the moment would be lost and she soon would be gone.

The next place was superb. Built by a Modernist architect in the fifties, it comprised a series of interlocking rooms that seemed to float from sheer partitions. Two silver pools ran down each side and an Oriental garden flanked the others. William couldn't disagree with Bunny's proclamations that it was "one of a kind," and "chic in a Zenny kind of way," and mentally installed himself, padding his way kimono-clad to an uncluttered desk, alternately swishing about in the pools like a koi. He was disappointed when Madeline nixed it. "I don't know—it's kind of cold. All that glass and concrete would make me feel exposed." William glanced at Bunny, who returned a look. *She's making a terrible mistake.* For a moment he and Bunny were bonded: clearly being a celebrity Realtor wasn't as easy as it looked. At least William was starting to understand what Madeline might be looking for: something traditional and private. Comfortable, but not fussy.

The last home of the day, a "classy Cape Cod," on the market for the first time in its fifty years, seemed to satisfy all Madeline's requirements. Bunny's prognostication that it would be "The One" proved more prescient than William's initial skepticism had allowed. The seller, the widow of an old-time Hollywood producer, had been shipped out by her children, but there was enough of her spirit in the garden of lilac and hydrangea, her clapboard and picket, to know it was a place that had been lived in and loved. The bedrooms had all the original drapery: all flounces, flowers, and old quilts. The library, full of first editions of Hammett and Chandler, had a secret wall that concealed a projector for a quick transformation into a screening room. Madeline asked Bunny about installing security cameras around the perimeter—*no problem*—otherwise, Madeline seemed satisfied by the thick stucco walls surrounding the property.

When Bunny finally left them alone to soak up the atmosphere, William and Madeline wandered around, suddenly aimless without her guidance and strictures. They went out to the garden and meandered along a maze of gravel paths emanating from a sundial in the center. They stopped every so often to speculate on the herbaceous borders—it soon became clear that neither of them knew much about plant life or gardening. All William knew was that the garden was mature, more Mediterranean than Cape Cod,

and that it was good to be up in the hills. The scent of jasmine
hung heavy in the air. The temperature had climbed and his back
and arms were starting to prickle. The idea of pulling off his shirt
and diving into that sexy kidney-shaped pool on the other side of
the house seemed like a good one.

In his dreams maybe.

She was walking slowly. He hoped she would take her time.
They were done playing house. The question was how to prolong
the moment. With a dinner proposal or invitation to see a movie?
For a movie star, the latter seemed banal, the equivalent of asking
a baker out to dinner to eat bread.

They reached an arbor of bougainvillea, a shock of saturated
crimson at the end of the garden, and paused there a moment.
William reached into the mass of flowers, absently pulling at the
papery petals. He immediately felt a sharp, stabbing pain. The
flowers were full of thorns—*how was he supposed to know?* He'd
jabbed his thumb and index finger right into them. There was a
metaphor in there—he didn't want to think what it might be. He
resisted the urge to suck his fingers and draw attention to his
stupidity.

"That must have hurt." She winced.

It seemed as good a moment as any to say something about
meeting again. That, or lean over and kiss her.

He caught her half on her cheek and the corner of her mouth,
but she met him with lips, so soft and sensual.

He was throbbing for her.

She was sublime.

The first time Bree saw Dennis, livid and sticky right out of the birth sac, she thought he was the most beautiful creature she had ever seen. In his crumpled gaze, she saw wisdom and hope. In his pronounced cranium, she saw a smart intellectual in the making. But as Dennis grew from chubby baby into cave-chested third grader, the difference between him and other boys his age who could throw a ball or write wobbly cursive became distinct. Bree was forced to see that a large head didn't necessarily mean a higher portion of coordination or social grace. Her observation was compounded by his teachers' observations about his insularity and lack of participation. The example always given was that it took several prompts for him to use his words. While his teachers acknowledged that Dennis was more advanced and better behaved than most, the problems they believed were ones of attention and sociability. It was said that left to his own devices, Dennis would go the entire day without talking.

Such was the level of concern that the principal of Mojave Elementary insisted that Dennis be evaluated by a developmental psychologist, making it necessary for Bree to take the day off work and drive all the way to Lancaster for hours of tests and brain scans—what she later came to call the "day of nonsense." It came as no surprise to her that the doctor's diagnosis—*autism this, Asperger's that*—was given with so much doubt and generality that she was skeptical that this so-called expert knew anything at all. For all his early years, really right until he was twenty, she had no problem getting Dennis to listen. *Go to bed. Brush your teeth.* He never gave her any trouble. He always kept his toys and pencils in good order and his handwriting mattered less once he was allowed to do his work on the computer. The fact that he could run circles around his peers in the hard subjects of math and science and read books about ancient mankind was evidence enough that Dennis needed no therapy. For the rest of it, Bree was content to hope for the best and pray. The days that were bad were the ones they played dodgeball: Dennis never would get out of the way. Fortunately the Lord showed his mercy. In five years, Dennis only got one concussion, and even then he seemed happy enough to get out of doing sports.

That her son should be different came as no real surprise to Bree. She thought that all Dennis's indomitable traits had been inherited directly from his grandfather and grandmother on the female side, with the circumstances surrounding his birth compounding his individuality. She saw Dennis as the product of fate and potent DNA that had collided to make one incorrigible whole. As for her own role in his creation, she couldn't recognize any part of herself in him at all. How she came to be mother to a special child was a source of constant wonder to her. When she tried to understand how this came to be, she would look back and try to remember her old self, the fearless and headstrong girl of her youth. When she did that, she would always come up against the gloom-cast figure of her mother, and she would try her best to understand her too, a supreme act of imagination and compassion in itself.

Theodora Hake worked all her life in a food market outside Baton Rouge. She'd started there as a bagger at the age of sixteen, risen through produce by nineteen to become manager, all in the course of two decades. The store was owned by an illustrious family, the Du Plees, who had made their fortune selling armaments. As well as owning thousands of acres of land and two gun factories in the southwestern part of the state, it was rumored that the Du Plees owned most of the town as well.

Theodora Hake was as dour as her daughter was optimistic. Theodora believed that life was harsh and unforgiving, whereas Charlotte, as Bree had been christened, thought that it was more a question of attitude and the rebound effect of what you put out there into the ether. Charlotte came to see this after so many years' witness to her mother's joyless existence. She figured there was a link between her mother's outlook and her life's poor and mournful quality. Her mother must have chosen to wear the garb of one of life's unfortunates because it suited her personality, which was cold and unloving: gray is for grim.

Charlotte was not like her mother. She wanted to paint life with another palette, using vivid colors and only happy ones. A persistently cheerful nature told her that if she looked on the bright side, things would always work out for her, as sure as she was that yellow was for sun.

Charlotte and her ma lived in a tract house, two doors away from the store. It was noisy right there on the main road, and sometimes Charlotte found it hard to sleep. The neighbors made such a rumpus at night with their strange howls and cries that Charlotte was grateful for the metal grids incarcerating all the windows and doors. However, the location was convenient enough: it was near enough for Charlotte to walk to school and her mother to walk to work; that way they saved money on gas.

Charlotte couldn't remember any childhood outside the store. Her first memories were of bright cereal packets and the eye-pricking disinfectant they used for swabbing the floors. With the skyscraper towers of boxes in the storeroom as her playground, the supplies became her toys. There were coffee stirrers that spilled into pick-up sticks, and napkins that transformed into a fleet of magic carpets, poised to fly at her behest. Her most vivid memory was climbing up the counter and scalding her hand on the hot dog grill. Her mother had to close the store for the lack of supervision and drive Charlotte twenty miles to the nearest hospital, the local doctor's rates being too dear. During the interminable drive, the fire raging in her hand, Charlotte was rebuked for her selfish behavior. Mr. Du Plee had been so good to them, giving employment to a woman with a child and no husband—and there they were letting him down. To stop herself hollering with pain and further enraging her mother, Charlotte cast around for the bright side in the situation. She found it there in her mother's disappointment, like light itself—the sunburst of lines radiating out from her puckered mouth. The lesson she took from her mother that day wasn't so much to steer clear of hot dog irons, but that the Du Plees were more important than human health itself, which put them up there somewhere near God.

Mr. Du Plee only came into the store once. Charlotte remembered him because he was the only man she'd seen wearing a double-breasted suit like the ones she saw in movies. She noticed that her ma wouldn't look him in the eye, and she suddenly became uncommonly shy and girly, unlike her usual forthright self. It was also unusual that Charlotte was allowed to serve Mr. Du Plee. She wasn't normally allowed to deal with customers directly. Mr. Du Plee had asked for matches, fixing her all the while with a dull assessor's gaze. When he handed her the money, he let his manicured hand linger there in her palm. Charlotte saw how perfectly white the crescent moon was at the top of the pinky buff of his nails.

Then he took his change and went.

That was the only time Charlotte met her father. All Charlotte had ever been told about him was that he had been killed after her birth, when a car had careened out of nowhere, run him down, and disappeared back into the hellhole from whence it came. This information had been given her when she was two. The fact of it had been forever understood, so it was never questioned or deemed to be unusual, or even of particular interest.

The truth about her paternity was told much the same way as all the other lies: factual and simple, as if it had always been known.

Mr. Du Plee was her biological father.

Charlotte was a family name—Mr. Du Plee's favorite grand-mother had been called Charlotte.

Mr. Du Plee gave them money to pay for their modest life. The money—cash only—would have ceased if she'd ever told anyone.

When her ma finally chose to share the information, she was poorly, half-passed in the hospital. A tumor in her breast had brought about a devastation. Her body had wasted and her flesh had collapsed, becoming translucent, rivers of veins.

The news came as both a surprise to Charlotte and not one at all. The clues had been there all along. She just hadn't seen them. She felt as though she had been slapped into sense or stung by in-tense clarity.

She started to cry.

Her mother hissed, "Don't make a scene, girl," then sighed impatiently. For the last time it turned out. She expired after pass-ing on her burden.

Charlotte was sixteen at the time. With no one to turn to for advice or counsel, she went to the gates of Mr. Du Plee's mansion and rang the bell.

A white-jacketed retainer answered the door.

"Tell Mr. Du Plee his daughter was here today. Please tell him

174

that my mother is now deceased and—" She broke off. Her attempt at a dignified statement had gone sharp, into a high-pitched squeak. Clearing her throat, she tried again. "Tell Mr. Du Plee I won't be needing his hush money because I'm going to California. And make sure his wife overhears, won't you, please?" Then she turned and ran away, not before seeing light dancing in the manservant's eyes. Judging from his reaction, Charlotte thought there was a good chance he would do her bidding, and it was an additional comfort that he might take pleasure in doing just that.

Charlotte hitchhiked all the way to LA with her school friend, Treya Parnel. Unlike the other girls at school who were drab and boring, Treya was a lively spirit who shared with Charlotte the same sense of adventure that transcended the small-town view. Together they had the guts to make faces during the principal's Presbyterian dronings. Together they drew obscenities on the walls in the girls' locker room. Together they had made a pact to leave as soon as the opportunity presented itself. They'd been infected by a mood they'd heard was sweeping across the country. There was music on the radio that stirred their souls: idols Jagger and Morrison to be adored. In magazines they saw pictures of a golden, freer place. California beckoned as their promised land.

They were only half a day away from their destination when Charlotte first saw the soft ocher of the Santa Rosa Mountains. It was dawn and the first glow of light seemed to be casting magical rays of welcome and invitation over her. Under this spell of sunrise, Charlotte Hake had the first of two epiphanies. (The second would be the greater, but she would have to wait several years for that.) Charlotte had the driver stop so she could get out and kiss the earth, and declare herself Charlotte Hake no more. The name Charlotte didn't belong to her, it belonged to Mr. Du Plee. She wanted nothing more from him so hereto she would call herself Bree. Bree was a better name, more in keeping with her new life and her aura, which she had been told by a roadside tea-reader was as full of sunshine as her hair.

In Los Angeles they waitressed here and there, slept with a lot of guys, hung out on the fringes of the scene. Treya even did a bit part in a movie—*Babe on a Bike*—but her career as an actress didn't pan out. Six years later, after all the partying, the ever-changing digs and breaks that hadn't come, they decided to move on. A waitress friend had told them there was work to be had in the beautiful new ski lodges at Mammoth Mountain. It didn't matter that neither of them had seen snow or ever skied. They headed north, stopping to eat breakfast at a brand-new Denny's coffee shop on the Mojave 14 intersection.

Minutes after finishing the last hash brown, Bree was doubled over with pain—the butter was rancid, she was sure. Whatever the cause, the manager took a shine to her and offered her a job. She stayed for thirty years.

"The rest was history," she'd say with a laugh. "Must have been the sight of me heaving with my butt in the air. Now that's the bright side for you."

The manager didn't expect much in return, only the liberty of making a few suggestive remarks to her in the condiments cup-board. After serving waffles to his wife and bonding with her, Bree was empowered, and the manager ceased the talk. An early coro-nary saw him off and Bree cried at his funeral.

Denny's had been built only three years prior, and it still had the luster of a new place: gleaming chrome and Formica that smelled of new plastic—and the jukebox had all the latest hits. Back then it was the only coffee shop on the strip. Since then a

Fatburger had sprouted up, and a doughnut shop that served lousy coffee. Three gas stations followed, a Jiffy Lube, and a Tiresforless. What had been an empty highway became a thriving thoroughfare. When Bree decided to waitress there, she figured she had job security because travelers on 14 would always be in need of a cup of coffee and a smile. She was right about that. Denny's had endured. Sometimes she wondered what would have happened if she hadn't met Boris. Probably she would have followed Treya all the way north. But when she replayed that night, it had a sort of fatality about it, as if her life could never have been any different.

One night, and her future unfolded there on Boris's passenger seat.

Boris was a trucker with gold teeth and straw-colored hair.

Hello Hunky, she'd said to herself when he sat down at her booth, all muscle and glinting smile.

After mopping his plate clean (on her recommendation he'd chosen the Sunshine Breakfast), he'd called her "princess" in a heavy Russian purr and told her he'd been looking for a good woman all his life. Now he had found Bree, he wanted to marry her.

Now truly, that was a proposition.

Hello, I love you, won't you tell me your name?

She met him that night in his snug cab. He laid a fur rug down on the seats and made love to her. In all her fucks—and there'd been a whole lot of them—she'd never known such pleasure. It didn't matter that his breath was stale and stank of liquor, or that the sum of his conversation was a series of grunts. He made her come, and come again. When he took off in the morning, he told her to be good and promised to be back in two weeks, after depositing his load. He kissed her, glinted once more, and then he was gone.

And so Bree waited.

She waited and waited.

Then waited some more.

She never doubted that Boris would come. He felt significant. She didn't know how, but in one sense she was right. Many months later, mid-order (a cantankerous customer insisting he'd asked for the Sunshine Breakfast when he had not), waves of dizziness and nausea swept over her and blood came flowing out, pooling beneath her on the linoleum. She was rushed to the hospital. And then:

They cut me open and took out a baby.

Hallelujah.

Boris didn't come, but the Lord did instead.

She'd denied her pregnancy all those months and neglected to nourish her swelling body. Her muscles had wasted and her legs had got skinny. She'd thought it was from walking the three miles to work every day and back at night—no wonder she'd felt tired. Yet the baby had grown fat, sapping the goodness from her bones.

It was a miracle.

When the nurse asked the baby's name, Bree stammered, "Denny's."

Seeing the nurse's amazement, she quickly amended his name to Dennis.

For all Bree's hopes and prayers, the years went by, middle school through high, and Dennis never integrated with his peers. His behavioral tics continued to set him apart, and it didn't help that physically he stood out a mile from the others. It wasn't that he was bad-looking: with Bree's pale blue eyes and lashes as thick as a cow's, his features were really quite attractive—except perhaps they would have looked better on a girl. As he grew, his body remained slight and never quite caught up with his head. A slight stoop in his shoulders gave him the appearance of being doubly burdened. When Dennis walked, he took small cantering steps, and he always approached his destination sideways like a crab. His unique way of moving was born of caution: it was his way of assessing the situation in advance of his full-on physical arrival. For all the mocking talk about Dennis—and there was a lot over the years—he didn't seem to care what people said. His lack of concern was his armor, protecting and deflecting all slights flung his way. Eventually, the kids at school gave up teasing him. It was boring trying to provoke someone so completely unresponsive. Dennis became accepted as part of the scenery: *Frankenstein. Dufus. Whatever.* He was always useful to compute a math problem and call out the answer without looking up.

The truth was, Dennis had better things to think about than reacting to silly comments.

There was the universe, so big and infinite, which he experienced as a series of pulsing connections that sometimes shocked like electricity in his brain. When he saw a student spitting obscenities at him, Dennis saw them as an anthropological speck, the offspring of a generational mutation that went all the way back to the most significant time of human evolution, the first moment of conscious thought when man was able to distinguish himself apart from other animals. He could trace his tormentor's shortcomings all the way back to his ancestors and satisfy himself that such pre-Neanderthal behavior was because his predecessors were the last to make that great leap and separate themselves from apes.

All this mental activity could be overwhelming, loading each encounter with the baggage of generations past. Dennis could almost see them flicking by, a Rolodex of dead persons speeding backward through the centuries. More often than not, it was easier for him to switch off and go to a quiet place within himself, one that brought him both peace and calm. As for his own position in the big picture, he had so little sense of self he might as well have been pure circuitry—although for practical purposes his mother was the boss of him. That much was clear.

Of the two pastimes that compelled and absorbed Dennis, his favorite was playing with Madeline Brook.

Madeline Brook was the town he had slowly been building over the years. He had recently named it after a girl, after being shown her picture in a magazine: a cowgirl in chaps, with a lasso and go-getting smile that seemed to embody his town's spirit. He'd liked it so much he'd used the picture to make a billboard for the entrance: WELCOME TO MADELINE BROOK. As Dennis had just made a stream alongside Main Street, it occurred to him that Madeline Brook was a good name for his town.

Madeline Brook was Western, with stalls and horses and saloon bars; it had been updated and expanded since the Gold Rush and now had two gas stations, restrooms, and a fleet of Cadillacs. When he wasn't at school, he was collecting and constructing, scouring catalogues to keep abreast of the latest developments in architectural styles. After Dennis's first kit, when Bree saw the focus he'd brought to gluing, his hand-eye coordination not much in evidence anywhere else; she encouraged his interest with more purchases and subscriptions to specialist magazines. They only came into conflict over Madeline Brook once, when the town pump went missing and Dennis insisted it had been sucked up inside her prying vacuum nozzle. Bree was forbidden to clean his room unsupervised. The sight of her little man crying his heart out was enough to make her abide by his rules.

His other interest developed after a digital camera was left in one of the booths at the restaurant by a tourist. After a month, the forgotten property still unclaimed, Dennis was allowed to borrow it with the proviso that he never take it to work. Since leaving school, he'd taken a job at the car wash and had his Swatch stolen straight from his arm. Bree wasn't letting him take any chances with someone else's belongings.

Outside of work, Dennis was rarely separated from the camera. The lens became the way through which he viewed the world, removing his subjects from a confusing infinity of associations. Contained in the frame, Dennis could approach his subjects head-on and capture the moment in its pared-down simplicity. After a couple complained about being recorded, Dennis was banned from shooting customers. (Marge, the waitress, said the couple was embarrassed about being caught talking with their mouths full.) At least Dennis was able to find more compliant subjects among the still lifes of the Sweet'N Low packets and in the company of those who worked shifts at the diner.

M arge was his leading lady. Large as life, she filled the screen with her voluminous cheeks and guilty eyes. A perpetual dieter, Marge used camera time like a WeightWatchers journal, recounting her day's intake and high-carb slips.

"I've been bad this morning. Two Krispy Kreme doughnuts on the way to work and I'm seriously contemplating the mac 'n' cheese for lunch." Like her customers, Marge drew the line at being filmed when eating. She was trying to educate herself to treat food with respect and approached meals as if they were sacred.

His other subjects were the cooks, and brothers, Santos and José. They'd pretend not to see Dennis when he'd sneak in the kitchen and curl knee-level on the shelf, allowing him to film their checkered pant legs going from grill to plate, moving hash browns to serving hatch. When Dennis revealed himself they'd shout: "Whoa, Meester Invisible. You scared the sheet out of me!"

At night, through trailer walls that weren't much thicker than card, Bree could hear him making home movies.

This is my shoe.

These are my pajamas.

In a Dada-esque moment, Dennis might add:

This isn't my shoe.

These are not pajamas.

Bree didn't know what he was talking about. She didn't know he was talking molecular deconstruction.

Being Dennis's mother never tested Bree's faith, but it did test her belief in the right to live in perpetual sunshine. Once Dennis started school, it seemed that a cloud of worry had settled over her and refused to budge. It stayed there through graduation, hanging over her as she watched him approach young adulthood. It wasn't just his sparse monologues or the tap of plastic hooves that kept her awake at night, it was the question of what would happen to Dennis once she was gone.

On the bright side, Dennis had held down a job at the car wash for three years and been promoted to rigging vehicles for smog checks, so her son's security was in some way improved. On the overcast side, she couldn't see much room for career advancement, and it didn't make the idea of his cooking a home-cooked meal any less worrying. She would always fear for him around a naked flame. She would always have to wonder about his chances of meeting a nice girl, someone who would one day let him know the everyday miracle of becoming a parent. Such mortal thoughts dogged her in the shadow of her mother's death. As much as Theodora had seemed like an old lady at the time, Bree realized that her mother hadn't been much older than she was now when Theodora had died. While Bree considered herself in rude health, she also knew that nothing could ever be taken for granted, especially when it concerned the vagaries of God's will.

As mellow and providential as Bree tried to be, whenever she saw Dennis being ostracized by his peers, she couldn't stop unhappy thoughts from building up like sediment in her heart. With every slight against her son, another layer of bitterness formed, weighting her down, making her heart turn that little bit harder.

Throughout his school career, Dennis wasn't invited to any

social events outside of school. Not one sleepover, party, or playdate. Bree tried to remedy this once by inviting his class for dinner
at the restaurant. It was a fiasco. Ten boys showed up—all the
wrong kind. They were rough and rude; interested only in how
much free food they could eat. They paid no attention to Dennis,
who disappeared into the kitchen to watch milk shakes churning
in the blender.

Bree snapped. She threw them out, bad words spewing.

I'll tear your greedy throats out.

The boys didn't care. They were laughing as food spilled from
their mouths; they had grabbed their burgers and were still eating
as they ran. Only later did Bree understand that Dennis's having no
friends had allowed her to avoid the troublesome issue of outside
influences on her son. Although for many years it had been bitter,
though she hadn't realized it at the time, it had also been sweet.

She saw this when Roy Snicks moved in five plots over, and
Dennis started spending so much time with him.

At first she didn't mind. Roy was always affable. *Hi to you. Well
hello, Mrs. So and So.* He was the mailman so he always knew everybody's names. He didn't seem like a queer—only a friendly type.
He was the kind of person who was nice to everyone. It was Roy
who turned Dennis on to the fan magazines, including the one in
which Dennis first saw Madeline. Roy had the nerve to tell Bree
that it was love at first sight—total bull—when Madeline was just
another tight-assed girl in a magazine. They were a dime a dozen,
as she and Treya had found out the hard way. It bothered Bree that
Roy seemed to be fueling her son's interest in the bimbo, making
him look at pictures and indulging his schoolboy fantasies. The
worst of it was that she could see her son changing under his influence. He had become more secretive, less open to her. She could
feel a distance growing between them, and the person causing that
divide was Roy Snicks.

When Roy arrived at the RV Park from Reno, Nevada, he had been in California only two weeks. Most of that time had been spent on the road, zigzagging across the highway, zagzigging across county lines. Roy liked to drive long and hard: sometimes for eleven hours straight. To him that was like the perfect one-night stand: no rest, a feat of endurance, followed by the satisfaction of leaving before anything got in the way or, worse, disappointed. Roy had been itinerant most of his life. He never stayed anywhere longer than a few months. A few months was all he needed to get his shit together and recharge his batteries before hitting the road again.

Roy always traveled light. One bag, a vehicle, a little food and water, and some "happy dust" produced by the occasional injection of cash.

Now cash, or the getting of it, could be a problem when a new town only sometimes meant a new job—if he could nail a new ID and a social to go with it. There were times when he came close to folding, but somehow at the last minute Roy Snicks managed that extra win to stay in. He did this by keeping his tricks small, banking on the fact that petty crime was so prevalent that if you left your window open or allowed yourself to get scammed, you were the stupid one and no one bothered to investigate. Roy stole and sold cars when and if he could, but the ones he drove were always legal. Driving a stolen car was as good as walking down the freeway with a red flag strapped to his butt. License plates were always the first thing the cops checked. Whatever he was, Roy Snicks wasn't stupid. When he could get it, Roy's occupation of choice was postal work: out of every sack that went missing in his care, there was always one piece of information to be mined. With his gift of gab, one piece of information could be parlayed into one piece of gold.

He had chosen Sonny's RV Park because he could rent by the month and it was dead. Just fat people squeezed into picnic chairs and the static of TV coming from inside their trailers. He took it as a good sign that the play area was empty and rusted over. Roy had grown up under crazy duress: one of eight in a one-bed apartment. Nothing bothered him more than to see a woman with more kids than sense. And he didn't like kids, period. He didn't like the way they looked at him, unsmiling, beady eyes implying an unspoken demand. Their ability to multiply in hostile conditions was akin to rats or other vermin. In a perfect world they were good for one thing—a visit from the exterminator.

The exception was the retarded boy at Sonny's. This boy was a good listener. He disagreed with nothing and he never asked any questions. Roy could spend hours hanging out with him without having to listen to any stupid conversation. Roy liked the way the boy would let him be. The boy turned out to be useful when Roy was low and needed that little something extra to pick himself up and get happy.

He discovered something else about him when they were sitting on the swing set, and Roy was reading a magazine.

Would you look at this piece of ass?

Normally when he said something Dennis would stare. Roy could say, *Want a doughnut? The sky is blue*, or, *This place sucks* three times before he'd catch Dennis's attention. Then he'd look at him as if Ray had said something amazing.

This time Dennis started shaking. He was shaking so much Roy thought he was having a seizure. He'd heard about seizures. He'd been at a gas station when the attendant had gone down frothing. He'd been told by the boss that the boy was epileptic, considered by Indians to be a gift from the gods, or something like that.

It was only when he saw the bulge in the boy's pants that he understood what was happening.

From then on, Roy knew his weakness and how to play him.

He started slowly, making sure that he didn't overdo it and arouse suspicion by charging too much. He knew the boy's mother wouldn't allow it. She was a bad combo of fierce and cheap.

Roy would go to town, download some photographs at the copy shop, scribble a signature and, *bingo!*—seven dollars right there. It was enough to keep him in business.

It was twenty dollars for a fan club fee.

Fifty for her address.

One hundred and fifty for door-to-door service to her home. That was sweet, because on the weekends, Roy liked to party. He didn't care how far he drove as long as there was the chance of some world-class pussy the other end. After the first trip, door to door became door to the bottom of her hill. He made Dennis walk the final leg because he was busy and had things to do. Roy would drive to town, leave Dennis at the pillars to the Doheny Estates, drop down to the strip. He'd go to the Whiskey-a-Go-Go, pop a little Ecstasy in the boys' room, dance like crazy with the object of creating maximum contact with the chicks with the biggest sets. Only in the morning would he remember Dennis, then he'd drive back to the Doheny Estates and see him standing there exactly

187

where he'd left him—at the bottom of the hill outside some motherfucker's Tudor château.

Sometimes, when Roy saw Dennis waiting, all patient-like, he'd get a lump in his throat. He was moved by himself: his own capacity to be moved, and his own generosity that he was helping this sad fuck to pursue his dreams and get a life.

What he remembered about their first year of marriage: the heady disbelief that access to her had been formalized and sanctioned.

Tenderness and awe that such intimacy could exist between man and wife.

The discovery that their Dream Home needed untold sums of money to renew its old-world charm.

The trial of living in a building site; *ergo*: gratitude for his day job. The company of Donne and Shakespeare and bright-eyed students was a welcome escape from dust and drilling and muffin-topped builders.

And the night job was nonexistent, especially when Madeline was around. She liked to stay in and cook elaborate meals. She liked to watch documentaries, the more earnest the better. She wanted to have sex—he never could argue with that. Given the limitations on his day, these cozy evenings sometimes felt like time away from his book, but then Madeline was so much his inspiration, he could look at their time together and justify it as research.

In any case, six months of that year, Madeline was away filming. William flew in to visit her on location, never staying longer than a few days. Passionate reunions in Toronto hotel rooms were all very well, but visits to the set were less satisfying. The set was a foreign court, a fiefdom subject to unfamiliar laws and hierarchy. As far as William could tell, the studio was the oligarchy, subject to all the political conflicts of any bourgeois committee; the actors were royalty, worshipped and resented in equal parts, which left the crew in the class of glorified serfs. His nonstatus as a curiosity and outsider was confirmed by aggressive stares from everyone.

When Madeline was in town, Romy was never far. Romy was single, always available to drop by for a meal and lingering chats. After her initial hostility toward William, there followed an uneasy truce and the beginnings of an amity. William came to appreciate her perspective: a wry mixture of smarts with self-deprecating humor, sharpened on the edge of her own thwarted ambition. Romy came from a family of Jewish academics. She was the first in generations not to go to college. A natural comedienne, she entertained William with accounts of life as a personal trainer. His particular favorite was that at six every morning, five days a week, she went to a media mogul's McMansion to wait in the hall for an hour, only to be dismissed by him when their "workout session" was over. The said mogul would appear at the top of the staircase, Frette gown flapping to reveal a semitumescent penis. Like an aggressive prosecutor trying to trip the witness, William pressed her for details about what exactly she'd seen, but Romy never deviated from her statement. "It's always *semi*." Romy had arrived in LA around the same time as Madeline with the same purpose of being an actress. They'd bonded at a cattle call for a TV show, but whereas Madeline's career had evolved, Romy's had not. After three years of unemployment, she came to realize, "I couldn't fool myself anymore. Whatever my heart was telling me, it was wrong. Most of the time I was spending in the gym working out to keep myself *ready for that call*. Then I subbed a step class, took over someone's Abs and Buns. The day I admitted to myself that my acting career wasn't happening was as big as the first AA meeting for an alcoholic. When I could stand up and say, 'Hello, my name is Romy Rubin and I am a personal trainer.'"

What he remembered about their second year of marriage:
   Illness and doubt.

Madeline had been home only one night. The house was finished, restored to its former glory. William had deferred all decisions to her. It was her project-slash-brainchild, and she was paying for it. The result was a loving reproduction of the previous owner's décor that was, perhaps, a little too loving. William felt like a guest in a comfortable home belonging to some charming and hospitable friends of yesteryear.

The first evening had been spent talking about her experiences on the movie. She was glad to be done. The director was a *controlling pig* who had tried to micromanage her every move. Usually such a lack of collaboration would have undermined her, driven her to the point of crisis and tears, but this time she was able to detach and rise above it by focusing on the job for the sole purpose of getting it done. What happened to her on a movie set mattered less and less to her because she knew she was coming home.

"I was homesick for my foreman," she'd said with a kiss, prompting a lovemaking session there in the kitchen on their newly upholstered Pierre Deux banquette.

To her glee, William cooked supper in a hard hat one of the men had left behind, feeling improbably butch as he stoked up the BBQ for her favorite meal of grilled fish with potato salad on the side. Afterward, he walked around the house and watched her inspect the recently completed cabinetry. Her enjoyment was perfect. At that moment, he was happy to suspend disbelief about the decor. He would have suspended anything for another moment's ecstasy and to see her smile.

Her words on homecoming moved William to pull out his student bible, an old Oxford edition of the *Poetical Works* of John Donne, won in a school poetry competition. He read her "A Valediction Forbidding Mourning," and she cried at the imagery of the lovers as two legs of a compass with one fixed foot, that "makes my circle just/And makes me end where I begun." She said the lines were the most beautiful ever, but challenged the notion that death could ever be an expansion, even if it was spun "like gold to ayrey thinnesse beate." That felt too much like religious argument for her taste.

"You mean sophistry?" William suggested.

"Yeah. All we have is here and now."

William found such iconoclasm amusing, but had to agree. In months to come, he would look back on that evening as one of the last times they agreed about anything.

She woke in the early hours of the morning.

There's something in the bed . . .

The lights were snapped on, followed by a frantic search for an invisible invader.

But they could find nothing.

Madeline slept the rest of the night in William's arms, drifting in and out of sleep, only to wake periodically, swatting and scratching.

It's crawling, under my skin.

There were moments that night that William felt his skin crawl too.

First stop was Dr. Lipvitz, a dermatologist, who diagnosed a possible allergy. Tests were done. Cortisone prescribed for the intense itch. The results were inconclusive. The second opinion was from Dr. Ruziana, who said the same thing but took five visits to say it. William was irritated that he hadn't recognized the credibility of his office had been compromised the moment he saw advertisements for Botox and collagen-plumped lips in the waiting room.

Ruziana's successor was the charismatic Dr. Mayle, who operated from a Craftsman's house fifty minutes away in Santa Monica, thus breaking William's twenty-five-minute rule. William distrusted Dr. Mayle's subtle manner and guru-like qualities, namely his spry vegan appearance. He might have had more faith in his methods, a "fusion of *Chi* techniques" (as William called it, massage), if he had seen some tangible benefit to his wife's condition. Under Dr. Mayle's watch, the irritation spread from her arm to her neck, threatening to encroach on her face. Calls had to be made. Meetings and press canceled. The reason given: Madeline wanted to spend more time at home. *Hey, the kid just got married.* Perfectly reasonable if it had been true. William had tried flying a Madeline-needs-quality-time kite past Madeline's manager, Martha, only to be jerked down: "Honey, I have never met an actor who would give up a job to spend time with her family."

Martha drove straight over to the house and demanded to see Madeline. Only the sight of her client's excoriated skin gave her pause before she went into action. She got on the phone, researching the reputation of the different doctors. William could see the advantage of having someone on the team who was part hen, part rottweiler.

Martha's verdict: Lipvitz had a good reputation.

No one had heard of Mayle.

"Don't go out unless you have to. We don't need to tell anyone, nada, until we figure out what's going on."

The press became more aggressive, sensing a story. Madeline was snapped in the parking lot of a medical building in dark glasses, swathed in scarves, furtive and incognito. One look at her and it was obvious something was up.

It didn't take long for rumors to surface on the Internet.

Madeline Brooks health alert!

Miscarriage fears.

Breast implants for Maddy.

William knew this because periodically he'd surf the Web. Research pure and simple.

What exactly he was researching wasn't always clear. After grappling with his Madeline / William story, he'd put it aside. His characters were doppelgängers of living persons. Their literary transfiguration had not taken place. He could no longer fool himself that what he was doing wasn't a vile plagiarism of his own life. With her illness, he had to stop—to have continued would have been a vivisection.

And yet,

and yet . . .

Like an addict craving the thing that will destroy him, William kept returning to it in his mind. Even with characters with prospects as unfathomable as his own situation, he was compelled by the desire to keep writing. It was counterintuitive to put aside his best work when it was alive and flowing, quite literally, calling his name.

William forced a return to his janitor story and hammered out a new outline, trying to imbue it with depth and urgency. In the new version, John Moore, his sales executive and family man, discovers he is terminally ill. In the midst of a *crise*, he refuses treatment to prolong a life he doesn't value. He leaves his family to go work as a nighttime security guard/janitor in Manhattan's Diamond District. He chooses this job as an escape. With night

becoming day and no intruders for company, he can leave the
seclusion of his basement security booth at daybreak to sleep in
his studio apartment above a Korean grocery store and see almost
no one.

One evening John is at work in the booth when he sees a
woman on the monitor, shuffling down one of the corridors. He
has no idea who she is or how she got in. She's an old termagant,
devoid of past, future, or charm for that matter. John turns her out
onto the street.

But every night she returns, defying an elaborate alarm system
and all logical explanation.

John becomes accustomed to the sight of her. He leaves her
alone. She's homeless and doing no harm—all she does is rustle
bedding in one of the passages. He doesn't have the heart to call
the police.

He is on duty late at night when suddenly he has chest pains
and difficulty breathing.

The Termagant comes to his aid.

She takes him up to the street to breathe the night air. At first
he's reluctant to leave his post, but once he does he feels better,
somehow restored, and he's grateful for her help. A nightly ritual
develops. They go up from the basement to inhale the night air.
He comes to look forward to these outings, and they become longer and more frequent, and they go farther afield each time. Soon
she's taking him all over the city. They visit the rich and diffident
in sparkling towers, the lost and homeless in cardboard box cities.
Mysteriously, they find entrée wherever they go. He is aroused by
beautiful women in sex clubs; tastes fine food and wine in restaurants, feels pain and hunger on the street. He witnesses acts of
kindness and succor, and finally understands what it means to be
loved.

When he wakes every morning, he's not sure whether any of

it happened, whether it's a hallucination and the cancer has spread to his brain.

On one of these nocturnal reveries, he notices the Termagant seems to be changing. She is no longer the derelict and ragged person he first saw on the video monitor. She is metamorphosing into a lovelier form, with a beatific aspect that scares the hell out of him. It occurs to him that she might be an angel come to take him off. He is not ready to die. His energy may be dwindling but he isn't ready to go.

He wants to live.

They are out late when he finds himself at Grand Central station. They board an empty commuter train. He soon recognizes that it's the Harlem line and they are traveling upstate through Westchester. The journey is familiar. It's one he took countless times when he used to work in the financial district.

She's taking him home.

It's dawn when he arrives. He sees his wife inside the kitchen with their son and daughter. They are setting the table, making breakfast. They are bleary-eyed, he thinks from lack of sleep. It's unusual for them to be up so early. His wife seems aged by care. She's capable but weary, but she's carrying her years with dignity. His children are teens, hormonal and preoccupied. He can barely recognize them. They are changing so fast, morphing before his eyes. He sees that they are not the studious achievers he had once hoped they would be, but they're good kids and they're getting by. To have wanted more from them was ridiculous and vainglorious.

As he approaches the house, he sees they are grieving. He realizes they are mourning for him.

The man wakes. He is home in bed. His wife and children are around him, struggling in their various ways to let him go. He has never left them or the bed. The story is a morphine-induced tone poem.

William understood that this story was ambitious. It would be tricky to make a surreal landscape work literally and metaphorically, but there was something about his protagonist that haunted him—maybe he identified with his character's escapist dreams. In unfettered moments of confidence, William saw potential in the story, even fantasized about a movie sale. He imagined an Academy Award–winning, Tom Hanks tearjerker. A pumped-up distraction. The bottom line was that he needed to come up with something. Vivian had been calling. Over a year had passed since he'd received his contract, and he had nothing he could show for it.

She was driving on auto, already distracted by the prospect of the *vampires* waiting for her farther up the road. They were torturing her, bleeding her dry, making it a trial to go out— even worse to return home.

Staying in wasn't much better. Her housekeeper, Blanca, went around shaking her head and muttering prayers, and William spent most of his time closeted in his study as if she wasn't there. It was like being at someone's funeral, and discovering the person being mourned and missed was her.

Surreal.

If being a ghost in her own house was bizarre, it was even more so that she was adapting to her new persona. She slept more during the day, enabling her to stay up late and waft around at night. She avoided the phone and all contact beyond her immediate coterie. She had become a sad shadow of herself, hovering somewhere between what she used to be and someone she didn't recognize. Whatever she had become, she knew she sure wasn't living.

She tried not to blame William. She could see how hard it was to be around someone with zero self-esteem. She knew that the only thing that got her going was the idea of a new doctor: someone who would give a name to her illness. Someone who would find a cure.

And she was lonely without Romy around to make her smile.

For the first time in as long as she could remember, Romy was away and unavailable. She had grown accustomed to the uplifting quality of her self-dramatized angst: no matter how bad things were for Madeline, it was always worse for Romy. As luck would have it, Romy had gone to New York for six months to do a reality show, starring as a fitness dominatrix, charged with whipping a pack of schlubby New Yorkers into shape in time to run the New York Marathon. They had swapped calls, but Madeline hadn't persisted. She told herself that it wouldn't be right to risk bringing Romy down in her hour of triumph. Besides, she didn't much feel like talking.

Her thoughts veered to her mother and sister.

In all the turmoil, only one thing had become clear: a teary reconciliation with them was never going to take place. If there had been the possibility of anything she would have had it by now. If there had been something worth salvaging, she would have saved it. It was strange to think of them out there, going on with their lives without contact or connection to her. More and more milestones would pass: marriage, sickness, maybe even birth—there was still the chance she might get pregnant one day—and they would be the last to hear about it. Being severed from immediate family wasn't natural. She still couldn't understand what she had done to deserve it. Nothing. That was the point. Nothing. The injustice of it still caused a tightening in her throat. She told herself that she still needed to do more work putting them to rest. Bury them deeper in her mind. Easier said than done. They kept bobbing back up, forcing a dialogue in herself. Had she tried hard enough? Could she have done more? The answer was always no. Besides, her mother would have used her illness only to justify herself, because that was the kind of mother Fran was. And her sister was so weak it was pathetic. Brainwashed by Fran, co-opted as a depositary for all her rage. Fran had taken over her children because seven-year-olds were about her level. How dangerous and selfish was that? Shona could have done so much more. She was super smart, top of her class, yet she chose to get knocked up, marry, and divorce the first loser she met and stay at home instead. Maybe that suited her. Maybe she and Fran were perfect for each other. No wonder neither of them had . . .

By the time she knew what was happening, it was too late.

A *thud* against her door.

Too large to be an animal.

The car bumped over the grass and stopped inches away from a tree.

Deep red bark.

Please let it be alive.

Please.

The ground was spongy under her feet. It took several steps for her to realize that it was her legs, sinking beneath. With a sharp breath, she saw the figure was alive and weaving away.

That was ominous.

That could portend brain damage.

Wait, she heard herself cry.

The figure turned and looked back.

He was young. His youth was somehow shocking.

He started moving back toward her. His gaze and gait seemed to cut across the wrong way.

He lifted a camera to his eye.

He was photographing her.

Fuck. It's a setup.

The accident had been staged to expose her illness. Her scarf had dropped and he was videoing her neck.

Don't.

She lifted her hand as a shield, conscious of herself as a clichéd tabloid image.

But the boy seemed startled.

He scuttled to the side.

Then back across.

He was making his way to her on the diagonal.

He was holding out the camera.

Offering it to her.

She snatched the camera and was surprised to see that it wasn't recording. She turned it to playback and saw the last images were of an Asian couple outside the Egyptian movie theater on Hollywood Boulevard.

It took a moment for sense to return.

"We should get you to a hospital."

At the mention of hospital, he was off, galloping down the hill.

"Don't run," she cried. Her voice was shrill with panic. She was thinking about exacerbated brain damage again. "You need to sit down."

She saw him drop down on the verge.

He seemed to be waiting for something. She realized, for her next instruction.

"No, I mean . . . you can sit down at my house. Would you please get in the car?"

In the moments before she had invited him in, Madeline had made two split-second judgments.

One: he was well enough to wait to be seen by a doctor at the house.

Two: he wasn't a serial killer. It was obvious that he wasn't normal but instinct told her that he was benign. She had got that from the way he'd fled down the road and his dog-like obedience about sitting. The fact he hadn't tried to exploit the situation and run off to hire a personal-injury lawyer was a sign that he was as innocent and guileless as he seemed.

When they drove past the mob, she told him to keep his head down. He seemed to find this funny because he was grinning madly. After the electric gate had closed safely on the *bloodsuckers*, Madeline realized that she was smiling too.

How strange it was to be thinking of someone else.

At the point William was starting to wonder how little he knew Madeline, it became clear to him that he didn't know her at all.

There was her attitude toward the Psycho.

One look at him and William knew the type: dangerous and delusional. This one was apparently domesticated. William came home to find him sitting in the kitchen, drinking his tea with his wife. He knew that this young man had to be handled carefully. The last thing William wanted was to end up with a carving knife in the chest. William had to sit down, finger on the 911 button, and listen to a rap about ions and radiation—a ruse for not going to the hospital and getting an X-ray. Madeline looked on, serene as a Madonna, with a maddening smile he felt like slapping from her face. She kept nodding and saying it was a "miracle" that he was unharmed. It transpired that far from committing vehicular manslaughter, the only thing she'd hit was the jacket "Dennis" had been carrying.

Incredibly, she seemed to like him.

She even insisted William drive him to the bottom of the hill for his ride, where William waved *bye-bye*, knowing full well he'd be back.

Of course he'd be back.

He was a fucking stalker.

Then she found the strand in her neck. She'd extracted it from a blister, put it inside a sandwich bag, and presented it to William.

Now do you believe me?

The strand was black and wiry. It looked a lot like pubic hair. Isolated in plastic, it had the forensic look of evidence, as if it might hold a clue to her condition.

A conversation about how to proceed had quickly degenerated into a row, pitting the merits of the New Age therapies of Mayle versus the conventional wisdom of Lipvitz. William contended that Lipvitz's opinions took precedence over Mayle's. Lipvitz was a cancer doctor, for God's sake. He had degrees from every major university. "What lunatic doctor has a fusion method? Fusion in my cuisine maybe, but in my medicine? No."

Madeline was vehement. "You can't understand until you've actually experienced it. Something happens when I see him. Something shifts. You should try a session with him. It might help you—make you less angry."

Something about the anti-anger massage and her utter sincerity had made him chuckle.

"You can laugh, but he has the capacity to think outside the box—he's combined the best of Eastern medicine with the best of Western medicine."

"And the worst."

"I didn't know you could be such a prick."

William apologized for his disrespect before persuading her to let him take the specimen in to Lipvitz. She agreed, but only grudgingly, and with such uncharacteristic bad temper that William was provoked to react in kind.

The moment William had left, Madeline sank with the feeling she'd allowed something bad to take place between them. Without any pretense of self-respect, she'd lain down, submitted to his will, cast herself as a resentful patient with William as bullying nurse—easy to play when he was better read, better educated, better everything. But she was no idiot and she didn't know why she was allowing herself to be treated like one. She decided that the only way forward was to become proactive: to take responsibility for her health, which would stop this undermining dynamic from taking hold. She needed to educate herself. How exactly she'd do this, she didn't know. Presumably this was something she could learn too.

Somewhere she'd seen written, "Deterioration is fast. Change is slow." She'd remembered those words because they had struck her as being so true to life: a little bit encouraging, and depressing, all at the same time.

Yet it was incredible, the moment she put her mind to it, she was able to go out and discover a huge resource devoted to people such as herself—but she didn't have to leave the house or pay for a home visit. She had journeyed out into cyberspace, to the World Wide Web, and found whole sites devoted to her illness, continents of people with identical symptoms to her own. True to experience, there were fellow sufferers with a condition as tangible as the common cold, yet they were being treated by doctors, employers, husbands, and wives with the skepticism reserved for the man in the moon. She found a wealth of information, but no easy solutions and little agreement about the cure. Some claimed improvement through alternative medicine—homeopathy, kinesiology, Hopi Indian ceremony—only a few through the use of antibiotics. Some blamed emissions from big business, biochemical warfare, and a willful cover-up by the CDC, while others saw an epidemic and parallels between the denials of AIDS in the eighties. The only consensus was that black, threadlike extrusions were the norm, that public acknowledgment by the medical community was the first step in finding a cure.

Even without answers, Madeline was still grateful to encounter such online camaraderie. To find a support group was to be caught free-fall by a network of invisible hands. An hour in a chat room buoyed by messages of hope was more mood elevating than any drugs she'd been prescribed.

Fuck the doctors.

She wasn't taking it anymore.

When she tried to express this to William, she started to choke up, to well with repressed tears. In her effort to find words for her relief, to explain that she was actually as glad as she had been in God knows how long, she had tapped into a major reservoir.

His reaction was awful. He was cynical and patronizing, and he made no effort to hide it. He tried to throw doubts on everything. "These people promoting homeopathy are probably homeopaths." He referred to "cyber solidarity" as if it was a nasty constipating disease, and he blanketed her ideas with scorn.

Listening to him riff on the subject, Madeline couldn't stop the bile rising to her throat. For all the conversations they'd had since they were married, advice given, advice taken, sweet whispers, and cajoling words, she didn't want to hear another opinion from him now. She didn't want him to intellectualize anything or show her how clever he was. She didn't want him to say anything. She just wanted him to shut the fuck up.

And she said as much.

She also said that the only times she had felt any peace were in spite of him. Take his attitude to Dennis. She didn't understand why he would be so hostile to him. Dennis was way smart but clueless. He could talk about astrophysics but he couldn't walk up the street without getting knocked down. The times they spent together were such a great diversion when everything else was going to shit. Why couldn't he be glad? But instead he went off sulking for hours after his visits. Dennis wanted nothing. He was so easy to please and could sit for hours smiling at her collection of antique jelly molds. Where was the harm in that? Where was the wrong? She couldn't understand why he would take exception to such a sweet and innocent guy.

The only reason she could think of was that William was jealous.

Ironic, huh?

William left the room.

She heard his car, driving away outside.

Oh fuck off, why don't you . . .

She hoped the vampires would get him.

She found solace in the various messages waiting for her.

A Brit living in DC had adapted an old remedy for head lice and was having success with bathing in vinegar. Her husband said she stank of pickles, but she didn't care.

The bugs don't like it either! I'm so much better. The proof is in the pudding. I can go out without bandages, wear short-sleeved tops again. I used to be like an old dog scratch, scratch, scratching with fleas. I have my life back now—no thanks to any of those "health care professionals" who wouldn't give me the time of day. You have to wonder about these doctors, where their loyalties really lie. Is it with the patients, or is it with the drug companies that make them rich? I think I know the answer . . . If we try to heal ourselves we can put these crooks out of business. In my opinion that won't be a moment too soon. ☺

Mary Anne posted on madbutnotstupid.com:
The first step in my recovery was to get a big garbage bag and dump all the soap powders, the scrubbing agents, the toilet cleaners, even the toothpaste. Look around—there are chemicals everywhere. They're in our environment, our household products, in our food. They're full of carcinogens and are giving us cancer. What's the point of buying organic for our family when we have chemicals in every room? Are we all mad? It makes no sense. Do yourself a favor. Get rid of them.

Chemicals in every room.
In the manner of *Mary Anne*, Madeline went around, collecting the polish from the sideboard, the Windex and soaps from under the kitchen sink. She found disinfectants hiding behind all the S-bends in the toilets, and she black-bagged the lot. She felt a glow of righteousness deciding that Blanca would use only baking soda and vinegar to clean the house, even if they didn't do such a good job and the place was left not quite so clean. That would be a small price to pay for environmental purity. True cleanliness.
Her satisfaction was short-lived. She had the feeling that she had forgotten something. So she went around opening and closing all the cupboards again, scouring them for items that might have got pushed to the back and were lying there hidden.
It was difficult to see when there was so much *stuff*. Until then,

she hadn't even been in half the cupboards. After the move, Martha's assistant had come and unpacked and set it all up.

There were so many useless things just sitting there, *cluttering*.

A cocktail mixer.

Dump.

An old telephone.

Dump.

A basket of soaps shaped like cupcakes.

What the fuck?

Dump. Dump. Dump.

She had the nagging sensation she had forgotten something.

She couldn't think what.

Then she remembered William.

Maybe he was toxic too.

The bar was almost empty, too early for the professionals, just a man with an insinuating smile picking up a woman with sun-streaked tresses, coiffed to look as if she had just spent a day at the beach. Vivian sat alone and waited for William to arrive. It had been a while since she had seen him, even longer since she'd visited LA. She tried to imagine how he could fit into such a place. She couldn't, but then LA was elusive—so many atmospheres and surfaces that changed according to which way you looked, or the light. Vivian preferred her cities up-front. New York for its brash vitality. Paris, for its intoxicating elegance. London's staunch dignity was always reassuring. LA was too attractive for its own good. Prosperity that appeared effortless was a con. At least in New York you could see the honest grind.

If LA was a honey trap, drawing people in for a taste of the sweet gold, she suspected that William had fallen into it. With a moderate talent, he thought he would accomplish all just by wanting it. Now, with his silly movie-star marriage, his grandiose, alternately craven e-mails and procrastinating messages, it was clear that he was stuck. With every day that passed, it became more unlikely that he would be able to extricate himself.

There was a time that his failure to produce a manuscript would have been professionally compromising. Editors were only as good as their authors. A blocked writer was a liability, warranting damage control and a prescription of Ambien. Those days had passed. Some seismic shifts of her own had caused fissures between past and present, making her detach from current processes, editorial and emotional. She was fed up with authors' egos, authors' neuroses, corporate politics, the fine print, strained eyes, strained nerves, and was planning her exit from the company as soon as her contract was up. With only three more months to run, she was already halfway gone. Regarding William, she planned to assess the situation, make recommendations to all concerned, and nothing more. She owed this much to herself. As with so many adult situations, it was helpful to take an agnostic view. There was no right involved and certainly no wrong.

A useful maxim in more ways than one.

Especially handy at such a time as a pending divorce.

Irreconcilable differences.

The end of Bob and Viv.

Separation wasn't something she had ever envisaged. Granted, she and Bob had been having their different liaisons for years, but they were regarded as a form of brinkmanship: the courting of danger, followed by a quick retreat back into the comfort zone of their marriage. She believed this was what made it all work and kept boredom at bay, the usual death of most unions. With each dalliance deflected, their marriage became less susceptible to danger. It became stronger.

Except immunity is only immunity until weakness is exposed and someone goes down.

It was obvious when it happened. Bob was a terrible liar.

He always answered his phone. It was a fact of professional life that they were both hooked up to their BlackBerrys. The day he glanced at the number and let it ring, and returned it back to his pocket with a care that bordered on tender, was the day she knew something terminal had happened. Bob was never tender with his

BlackBerry. (She later accused him of looking like Marcel Marceau, cradling a cradle.)

The proof was found in his wallet.

A heart, cut crookedly out of red construction paper.

A child's valentine.

I love you, Daddy.

Bob had a six-year-old daughter. The child of another journalist, Susan Weiss, who orbited on the outside of their inner circle, or so she thought. Bob had found out about Allegra only a few months before when she developed type 2 juvenile diabetes.

Susan needs the extra support at such a difficult time.

Bob had no choice. He was Allegra's father. He now had new obligations.

Susan was recently divorced and lived only six blocks north of their apartment in the upper nineties. Allegra attended a private girls' school only three blocks south. Too convenient for comfort.

An affair she could have understood—she knew how that worked. Lies and obfuscation could be rationalized as survival mechanisms for the common good. But a child? Children had never been part of their planning. They had both agreed that gypsy journalists did not make good fathers and that Vivian was unfit for the messy trials of motherhood.

That the child might have stolen a piece of his heart—that part wasn't negotiable.

An avenue of escape opened up while pounding a quick six miles on the treadmill. She always watched TV when she ran. With a change of pace or elevation, she habitually flipped channels, using the stimulus to distract her from the ache across her lumbar spine. In recent months the pain had become worse, forcing Vivian to consult an osteopath who diagnosed "wear and tear" on her joints and advised her to look for a low-impact sport, one that would be less jarring to a maturing skeletal frame. To

Vivian a low-impact sport was an insult, an oxymoron really. Sport was all about impact: the building of fast-twitch muscle, the matching of an opponent, usually herself. She decided that she would rather run through the pain than join the undignified ranks of sprint-walkers who waddled their way around Central Park. If she became lame and her hips couldn't take it, they were redundant and she would get them replaced.

She was jacking up from eight to nine miles per hour, with a requisite flip of the channel, when her attention was taken by a raw-cheeked mountaineer on the Discovery Channel, introduced as a five-time Everest summiteer, Don Wilson, foremost guide in the United States, and so on. He was standing at the bottom of a former glacier, a melt of brown water and rocks, talking about the unpredictability of the weather systems. There were no longer seasons in the sense that he understood. With unstable conditions, there were new hazards for guides and mountaineers.

Vivian didn't hear the rest because she was seeing a project in him: an account of pushing rich clients and cappuccino-makers up the Big E. The story had a juicy human thrust. Talk about the ridiculous to the sublime. The guy had the potential to be the new photogenic Krakauer, the prospect of which carried her an extra six miles to an impromptu half-marathon.

With some perseverance, she was able to track Don down on a satellite phone, somewhere on a ridge in the Cascades.

He listened to her telephonic proposal before making it clear he had no interest in writing a book.

"I work from instinct, from a broad base of knowledge, but it's experiential, nothing that inspires a paper trail. My company is doing great. I started it from nothing fifteen years ago. My expeditions are filled to capacity—I have offices in three states and a hundred employees—that's not including yaks. I have thirty in Nepal. You have to understand there's only so many clients you can have on the mountain at one time. I don't need publicity for publicity's sake. I have good word of mouth and the Internet for that. I only use it when I need to get a message across. If you still want to meet, I'd be glad to tell you what I'm really about."

If having Bob and his new family on her doorstep made Vivian want to get away, Don's unusual offer gave her the impetus to travel cross-country to meet him in his Seattle office, a hub of equipment and smiling, apple-cheeked youths.

He greeted her from behind a disorganized desk: a jumble of PowerBars, free samples proffered from a tangle of crampons, permits, thermal cups, and carabiners. She saw immediately that the camera hadn't been able to capture his physical presence or his beauty. He was tall as an oak, with black eyes inherited from his Athabascan Indian mother and milky blond hair from his father, a trader from Talkeetna. His voice was low, so quiet that Vivian had to lean forward and listen more carefully—a subtle hook: behind all his soft-spoken charisma, she recognized an iron spirit, something implacable that demanded her attention.

Beyond the company, his guiding passion was a shelter for Native Alaskan women he'd started in Anchorage. The long history of displacement, overendowment by the land corporations, had led to problems within the native population. Unemployment and alcoholism were rife, as were rape and violence toward women. Victims were unable to seek justice due to conflicts between antiquated state and tribal laws. He had been lobbying with Amnesty International on this. The women were lost in the system, prone to depression and suicide. His mother had been one of these women. He was a child of rape. The shelter was something that spoke to personal experience.

Don's unsentimental honesty was impressive. Sentiment was overrated. There was so much time and energy wasted in a whining school of thought, a *wah-wah* culture that promoted a false sense of entitlement, unrealistic expectations that served only to perpetuate more misery. Vivian subscribed to the belief that unhappiness was an essential part of a child's development, a rite of passage that necessitated the escape and emergence from the parental swamp—the concept of "childhood" was a twentieth-century invention after all. Only losers got bogged down and were doomed to spend their lives wallowing in self-pity.

Don was clearly a winner.

He asked her if she climbed. He said she looked fit.

Vivian was thrown by his comment. The idea that he had been appraising her as a physical specimen all the while was disarming—there was even something a little erotic about it. When Don offered to take her out, she was secretly excited.

By taking her out, he didn't mean for a meal or date. He meant for a two-hour drive into the Cascades, with crampons, ice axes, subarctic down jackets, for some "basic training."

She was stunned by the crystalline beauty of the ice field, equally so by its physical demands. Light-headed with the altitude, the cold burning her lungs, she proceeded up the glacier kick-step by kick-step, following slowly in Don's trail. Every movement was a challenge for her, requiring frequent rest stops and a pace akin to slow-motion—no running here. The mountains seemed to reduce everything to basics. The need for fuel and warmth. The need to endure. She felt a preternatural calm.

She was making her way across the ice, when he caught her by the ankle and pulled her down. He was testing her reflexes for an ice-axe arrest, the only thing that would come between her and a slide to death into a crevasse. The proper action would have been for her to have whipped out her pick, hacked it into the ice, while simultaneously rolling her front chest and shoulders over it, with a slight lift of her midriff and stiffened legs, to create a body arc for immediate braking action with her toes—but she was many seconds behind thinking about doing that. She'd splayed on to her face. She'd been hyperventilating at the time, so her mouth filled with hard crusts of snow.

She could have been annoyed. Her heart was lurching. Her teeth ached from the cold. She could easily have chipped a tooth.

Instead, she started to laugh.

She was laughing because to fall without injury was funny.

She was laughing because she couldn't save her life if her life was at stake.

But she would try.

And this beautiful mountain man was the one to show her how to do it.

A week's climbing course culminated in an epic ascent of Mount Rainier—twenty hours in a blizzard—and a new ambition was formed. She would set aside three months for specialist alpine training, then she would climb the highest mountains on each of the seven continents: Elbrus, the Carstensz Pyramid, Vinson, Kilimanjaro, McKinley, Aconcagua, and Everest, in ascending order of altitude. The Seven Summits was already an established concept, but she would find her angle. Even if she didn't make it all the way, she would find success in adversity. She would find her limit. Her inner peak. She would write the book.

And she would do her best to sleep with Don on the way.

Naturally, she wasn't going to tell William any of this. An editor turning author was an apostasy. She couldn't expect him to understand, especially when he was going through such difficulties of his own.

She was surprised to find William so altered by his experiences. In the intervening months since their last appointment, he had aged dramatically. Everything about him now appeared to sag. His posture, inadequate at the best of times, was so poor as to make him seem positively homuncular: he spent most of the meeting slumped in his chair. His ego, always on the unhealthy side of healthy, seemed to have deflated to the point of humility. It was as if someone had come and popped his LA bubble.

To his credit, he was frank about his difficulties.

He had written himself into a cul de sac. He'd had to turn around, go back to the start, ditch the passengers, and find entirely new ones.

He needed a new deadline. Twelve months would be ideal.

Without making any promises, Vivian agreed to talk to the powers that be.

He might have to do an outline—if he would be amenable to that.

He agreed to do an outline, if necessary.

She told him she had to go to another meeting. A lie. She didn't want to get into a personal discussion. She didn't want to discuss her humiliating situation with Bob, and she didn't want to hear about Madeline—she could pick up *People* magazine if she wanted to do that. It was all so predictable and depressing.

She wanted to go back to her suite, maybe do some laps in the pool, which promised to be empty this time of night.

It was obvious that he wanted to go up with her. She could feel it in his hovering embrace.

But, no, that wasn't possible.

There was nothing aphrodisiac about failure.

William had never thought that a successful relationship should be predicated on a need for soul-baring candor. The idea that a spouse or partner had to possess everything, know every innermost, wart-filled thought smacked of emotional fascism and was morally repugnant. To leave some thoughts unspoken, preserve a degree of mystery, was as important and constitutional as the basic right to privacy.

William didn't think it odd or indicative of a growing divide that he hadn't been able to share his creative doubts with Madeline. He'd mentioned it once and found her fierce defense of him touching, but she was unable to say anything to persuade him that he wasn't rudderless up proverbial shit creek. He couldn't expect her to be objective or give a dispassionate opinion. What else was she going to say? A wife should never be called to testify. Soon, with all her dermatological problems, writer's block seemed rather esoteric, only one of many cankers multiplying in its host. The last thing he wanted to do was add to her burgeoning anxiety, so he never brought the subject up with her again.

If William had been able to practice a little of the objectivity he deemed lacking in Madeline, he wouldn't have been surprised to find that in a creative bind, his lecturing skills at the university were also compromised. It wasn't easy to deliver a speech on the metaphysical poets, to talk about muscular concentration of

ETHER

thought and use of conceit and commend the attention and rigor
demanded of the reader, when his brain was scattered, about as
intellectually rigorous as the young man who sat in class three
rows from the back, thumbing text messages on his cell phone.

He was rambling on about the use of the "extended conceit"
("one that sets itself the task of proving likeness") when he was asked
by a student to give a definition of conceit and provide one modern-
day example. As she looked as if she was twelve, he had to wonder if
she was one of those genius children who showed up to audit classes
from time to time. Trotting out his standard line that a conceit was
a comparison more striking for its ingenuity than its rightness, he
went on to give an example not half as sinewy as Donne or Dryden
but at least as personal. He likened his own dread-like nausea of sitting down to work every day to "morning sickness." Writing was the
"fecund body grappling with itself" and it wasn't always a "pretty
sight or feeling." The twelve-year-old remained impassive. The earnest students looked mildly concerned, and the texters (there were
several) continued jabbing away at their phones. What he didn't reveal was that with the passing of his deadline and his characters re-
fusing to animate, he was feeling more like a pregnant woman in
the early months of gestation, confronting the prospect of a miscarriage. In SoCal parlance, that would have been TMI—too much
information. Anyway, the conceit still worked.

No pregnancy is without risk.

The question of the risk-taking in the creative imagination was
one that endlessly fascinated him. In a discussion of experimental
art, the poet John Ashbery had asked: what if the drips of paint
on which Jackson Pollock had staked his artistic career had just
been splashes? The giant leaps of creation and explosion of conventional forms could have been a monumental gamble or folly, except
with Pollock's prodigious talent the risks taken only heightened

220

the excitement of his work, extended the boundaries of a dynamic genius.

What if it's just splashes?

A question he asked himself daily.

When William heard that Vivian was arriving in Los Angeles, she could have been the last of the big-shot gunslingers come to town to troubleshoot his cares away, he was that pleased to see her. Finally here was someone who knew the deal, who understood the stakes—a lot more than Paper House's modest advance. Bart Hopper had not come through with his promise to unlock Paper House's legendary purse. While he wasn't expecting Vivian to come and bail him out—he knew the rule: gamblers always gamble alone—William couldn't help but put his hopes on the outside chance she would try.

As it turned out, the meeting went as well as he could have reasonably expected.

She looked good, as poised and lovely as he'd ever seen.

She actually sat still. It was an old tease of his that she was hyperactive and needed Ritalin. She was always shifting in her chair, papers from lap to desk, desk to lap.

He accomplished part of what he'd set out to do, namely get her on board with the idea of the extension, plus he had all the catharsis of confession, the penitential satisfaction of coming clean.

When the meeting was over—Vivian restless again—William was suddenly seized by the impulse to tell her about his "other" manuscript, and found himself blurting out a description of his "intensely autobiographical piece. Very close to the bone, deeply personal—scenes from a marriage. It's probably unusable." He wasn't intending to show her the story. He just needed her to know it existed. By a dubious logic, he wanted her to know that his time hadn't been a total write-off.

Vivian hadn't risen to the bait but instead took him at his word. "If it's unusable, William, it's unusable. It doesn't matter how good it is."

Her reaction was deeply disheartening. William took it as a measure of his standing and decline. Vivian had lost interest in him and he was culpable. He hadn't helped matters—he'd been guilty of a teensy bit of playacting. He'd exaggerated a hangdog appearance in an effort to try to dramatize all his extenuating circumstances. He needed all the time he could get with the deadline.

It wasn't hard for him to play up the desperation.

He was desperate.

Only recently he'd gone to see Lipvitz with the mysterious strand. He'd sat in his lab, watching the good doctor squint at it under a lens. The suspense was unbearable. He'd known there would either be exceptionally good news or exceptionally bad. In an attempt to prepare himself, he'd made a mental checklist of worst-case scenarios that ran from drug-resistant tapeworm, through leukemia, all the terrifying way to HIV.

Lipvitz's conclusion was not on his list.

"I could send it out for a lab report but you'd be wasting your time. There's nothing there."

There's nothing there should have been good news, except the way he said it suggested otherwise.

"When you say 'there's nothing there . . .'?" William demurred.

"It's lint," Dr. Lipvitz replied. "No more alive than this microscope. Look, I'll be honest with you, there's a name for this: *hysterical parasitosis*. It's more common than you'd think. Whole

222

families come in. One person gets it and then they convince all the others they have it too."

William felt his shoulder itch. It was all that he could do to resist scratching.

"They come in with baggies like yours," Lipvitz continued. "They swear it's alive. Did you see it move, doctor? What I'm saying is that you need to go home to your wife. She doesn't need a dermatologist, she needs a psych doctor and counseling."

The truth of what Lipvitz was saying was undeniable. Profoundly disturbing. And sad. What kind of psychic pain would make someone invent an infestation?

All this William pondered over a solo lunch. After the appointment, he'd needed to sit down and he'd shuffled into the nearest restaurant. As he was on the Beverly Hills/Culver City border, the restaurant turned out to be full of industry types. He recognized two junior colleagues of Sue Black's, but to his relief they didn't know him, disassociated from his illustrious partner. Only after consuming half a bottle of Pauillac and a quarter of a steak au poivre did the pragmatist in William take control and figure out the probable cause of her ailment: stress. The probable cure: rest— along with some probable treatment from the head of the English department's wife, who he'd heard was an eminent psychologist. Exactly how he would present this to Madeline remained to be seen, but William still had confidence that reason would prevail.

As he'd watched people around him ordering food, making deals and talking, he knew his life had changed. He had entered a dazing new arena. His wife was sick and he was part of it. Just as he once had gone with her, intoxicated and swaying into a Palm Springs registry office, hand in hand with her he had joined the walking wounded.

Since that meal he'd become less hopeful.

Since she'd started all her crazy Internet networking. Whatever Madeline wanted to believe, all her new "friends" were a bunch of fully fledged loons.

He couldn't say he hadn't been warned.

Lipvitz had cautioned, "Whatever happens, don't let her go on the Internet. Now everyone's an expert, talking to each other, encouraging each other's fears. Before no one would take you seriously, now there's a world of people to talk to. Sure, they are victims of a disease, but there's nothing new about it. Mental illness has been around forever."

And yet William would have chosen any of her virtual friends over the presence of a stalker in the house. Since Madeline had started doing *projects* with him, Dennis was coming by most days.

They made jelly together using all twenty of her copper molds.

They did finger painting together.

They collected twigs and leaves and built a tiny town on the edge of the swimming pool. Madeline seemed especially delighted by this.

The more William pressed her for a restraining order, the more she seemed to welcome her follower. As William had made it abundantly clear he was unhappy having Dennis anywhere near the house, he had to wonder whether Madeline might be taking pleasure in his discomfort. Listening to her reckless laughter as she played kindergarten was infuriating enough, but her inability to see the precariousness of the situation, her total blindness, had William, once again, questioning her mental health. She didn't seem to see that the kid was one step away from a psychotic break.

It's a truth universally acknowledged that eventually everything turns up on the Internet. If you look hard enough, and you know where to look. A link to a link, to a link.

The proof he was looking for.

It was the work of an amateur.
The image quality was poor.
The hand unsteady.
The pale stare of the light a hypnosis,
the rest of the room in darkness.
Muffled traffic.
Ambient noise.
A slack voice, egging him on.
Show me the love.
The photograph on his lap was familiar.
The motion made it fall to the floor.
When he was done, he pushed past the camera.
His eyes, an animal's before slaughter.

Madeline had been around long enough to know that life could be cruel and unforgiving. She had seen enough unhappiness over the years to know that she couldn't expect to be exempt. The horror show of her parents' marriage had taught her that relationships were potentially scary and to be approached with caution. She had tried to create her own security by surrounding herself with like-minded friends and partners. Being with someone who was a kindred spirit, who could see her for what she was, not distorted through a shifting kaleidoscope of fame, was as important to her as sex.

She hadn't been with William long before the cracks in his confidence began to appear, revealing a more disjointed person than she'd previously understood. Soon these cracks widened to become gaping holes, allowing this other husband to emerge from the broken surface of his bombast and talk. For Madeline, it became a question of trying to figure out how to strike a balance with someone who was at odds with himself: a mixture of overbearing and remote, confident and not at all. Sometimes it was awkward because he didn't always judge things right. He wanted to be part of every conversation when it wasn't appropriate. He went around interfering in everyone's business, calling Martha to chip in opinions about projects and telling Blanca how often she should vacuum under the beds. Yet she tried not to let it embarrass or alienate her. His vulnerability actually deepened her compassion for him. It was all so human, this insecurity. It made her want to find a way through it to a place of calm. When she saw him struggling with his work, mooching around, never at his desk, she tried to reach out to him, only to be rebuffed. Years of propping up her father had made her a kind and patient caretaker, but William was different. Too proud to admit frailty, he had a way of turning everything around and making her feel as if she was inadequate for trying to help. When she became sick, she was in no shape to do anything other than look for new ways to cope and find comfort wherever she could get it.

The night William ambushed her with the tape, she realized there was a whole other level to his destruction. It was so much deeper and darker than she'd understood.

She didn't even look at him in case he was gloating.

Didn't want to give him the satisfaction of a reaction.

She told him that she was going to bed. She had a headache and would take a pill.

He didn't protest. He looked sheepish and morose—to her mind, a poor excuse for an apology.

She lay in bed with her eyes closed. She lay very still. Shock seemed to have immobilized her body although her mind was in a tailspin.

It was a while before William came upstairs and clattered in the bathroom. She could hear him rummaging in the drawers. She thought he might be trying to wake her to force a confrontation. She refused to engage. She had no sympathy for him. She despised his insomnia as the sleeplessness of a guilty mind.

Several hours passed before she could be sure he was asleep.

Sleep wasn't an option for her.

Not possible until she'd seen where else he'd been.

ETHER

She stole downstairs, a thief in the night.
 But he was the thief.
 A thief of trust.
 A thief of hope.
 She started with his e-mails.
 "I find myself thinking about you."
 He clearly had a thing about Vivian.
 "In all that has been going on, you are a beacon of sanity."
 Like he was married to Mrs. Rochester.
 Nice.
 Then she read his book.
 It took until dawn. It was two hundred and fifty pages.

Madeline was used to reading fictions about herself, stupid articles that friends sent, just in case she might have had the benefit of having missed them first time around. She tried to rise above mean-spirited trivia just as she did unfavorable reviews. She told herself that words didn't damage or define her, that anyone who tried to do anything laid themselves open to assassination.

Nothing had prepared her for William's quasi-fiction. To read it was an out-of-body experience: like looking down at someone who has the same life, same problems, through a funhouse mirror. It was disturbing that in his portrait of a neurotic actress, she could see herself and recognize the smallness of her life.

There was an exposition of their meeting, the heady beginnings of their affair. The fact they were mismatched was well-established. They both wanted something they thought the other would give them. He was brutal in his descriptions of himself and his failure as a writer whose only success had come through the chance discovery of the Péri diary. Within the confines of self-obsession, there was genuine affection there. He wanted to love her and she wanted to be loved, but that wasn't enough.

It never is, he'd written. An ugly self-fulfilling prophesy.

The betrayal was beyond. It defied all principles of intimacy. Most devastating was the note, jotted at the end.

Her beauty destroyed her family . . . ?

She tried to adjudicate this.

Her mother's unhappiness was there for as long as she could remember and surely predated her existence. Madeline and her father were the innocent parties; if anything, they were the injured ones. It was Fran's pathology that she chose to make a hell out of everything by resenting their closeness. It wasn't their fault that she and her father were so alike in their impulses and interests, both raw with feeling, wanting to go their own ways like beatniks or artists. Her happiest memories were of the ocean with him, making sculptures of seaweed and stone, paddling with boogie boards, later, surfing. If Shona wasn't included, it was because she kept having meltdowns about getting sand between her toes. She was frightened of waves and was always complaining. Were they so wrong to have left her behind? Had this brought destruction? Her mother was always mad at him for encouraging time-wasting pursuits when Madeline could have been usefully employed going to auditions or classes for "commercials acting."

You should be careful. A rash guard won't protect your face.

She'd made it sound like a threat.

By the time he'd decided to join Madeline in New York, any pretense of a marriage was over. And if city life didn't suit him, wearing a suit didn't suit him—it was because he should have been born before. He was such a fucked-up hippie. He called her *shaman*, his healer with magic hands.

He didn't die of a broken heart. He died of cirrhosis of the liver.

William—you have shattered more than you know.
Your book is shit.
I guess your last book must have been a fluke.
You are disgusting.
It's hard enough to think you've been secretly scribbling away,
exploiting me, exploiting my family—worse to realize that I
was a sucker for believing in you.
For believing in us.
That's the part that really kills me.
How dare you try and put your creepy spin on my family? You
hardly ever asked about them. You were never interested. I
remember you once saying, "What was Shona's grade point
average?" That was a classic. You were fact-checking, I see now.
I was crazy to have put my trust in you. I hate you for making
me feel this way. I can't believe that I ever . . .

She stopped.

She hated writing. Prose was too complex, too dense to penetrate. It was giving her a headache.

So she highlighted and deleted her words.

To say nothing.

How much more efficient that was.

That would say it all.

Originally the cops hadn't intended to arrest Dennis. They'd only planned to move him on with a warning. He was following orders to step away from the gate and he looked harmless enough. It was only after Madeline Brooks came out in her bathrobe and made a personal plea for them *not* to arrest him, insisting that they take him home to safety, that they'd entertained the idea of driving him anywhere. Madeline Brooks had been able to provide Dennis's address by directing them to the St. Christopher charm strung around his neck. It was engraved on the back with the words *God guide you home, sweet child.*

The cops told Bree that Dennis was placid at first. He'd only become agitated after he'd gotten into the squad car, when he'd seen the actress through the window going in the house. She'd looked as if she might be crying and this seemed to trigger his distress. That was when they'd had to restrain him. For his own safety and also for theirs.

Once he was home, his suffering was terrible. He'd pace around their small living space, baying every so often like a wounded animal. This caused problems with the other residents at the trailer park, as he was setting off the dogs barking, and the noise was driving everyone crazy. Bree feared that if Dennis didn't calm down soon, they would be asked to leave Sonny's, their home of twenty years. Then she didn't know where they would live or what they would do.

The only chink of light was that after Dennis's arrest, Roy Snicks had taken off, she hoped for good. She prayed that without his wicked influence, Dennis would no longer be tempted to go back and make a nuisance of himself with the actress. She hoped that the possession that had gripped his soul would release its hold and he would go back to being the boy he once was.

But that didn't happen.

He was never the same.

Dennis lost his job after repeatedly failing to turn up for work at the car wash. The manager was sorry to let him go. He'd always liked Dennis for being honest and, up until recently, a good worker, but given all his absences it wasn't good business to let someone so unreliable stay.

As Dennis could no longer be left alone, Bree had no alternative but to take him to work. It was lucky that everybody at the diner was so nice and sympathetic to him. Dennis was family. He had practically grown up there in the booths.

The new challenge was to keep Dennis contained in the kitchen with his frantic pacing, and safe from being scalded with hot food being passed around. This was a full-time occupation and there were times that Bree was so tested that she didn't know where she'd find the patience, the strength to go on. It seemed that God had abandoned her and that her prayers would never be answered.

Until his return.

She had waited so long.

His hair was silver now and if the truth be known, he'd grown a little porky.

She would have recognized him anywhere.

He sat down in the booth and she served him the Sunshine Breakfast, even though he hadn't ordered it. He seemed to find this funny. When he laughed, she saw his gold teeth had been replaced by dentures.

She joined him and sat close beside him, allowing her leg to rub up against his. He was glad the way only a man can show. He took her hand and demonstrated his gladness under the table.

She had decided to give herself to him one more time with abandon, and to wait until afterward to tell him the news.

She wanted pleasure first. After so many hard years, God knows she deserved it.

With the morning rush over, just a few stragglers eking out their time over refills, Marge and Santos in the kitchen with Dennis, Bree slipped outside to the parking lot.

He had a small flatbed truck, not the massive vehicle of former years. It had a musty tarp over the back, covering the mounds of grass and branches on the bottom inside. Bree supposed from this that he had exchanged long-haul for gardening. From her standpoint, a good development. With no transcontinental trips, he could stay nearer home and that meant they would be able to spend more time together.

There wasn't much in the way of talk.

He yielded to her body.

She to his.

Leaves and branches poking into her back.

Oh, how good he tasted.

Sweat and soil . . .

The residue of soap.

Then a terrible howl, and Dennis was there under the canvas. He was yelling at Boris, pulling him off.

Bree tried to cover their nakedness, impossible with boobs flapping like wings as she tried to find their clothes.

Baby, it's okay . . . baby . . .

Boris wasn't helping, jabbering *Dio* and *Madre*, as he scrambled for his pants.

She was barely out of the back when she heard the ignition turn.

She cried out, "Don't let him go, Denny."

Her eternal mistake.

Dennis was on him, throwing him to the ground. He was kicking him so hard in the back she could hear air wheezing from his chest like an old pair of bellows.

"Stop. Denny, stop. He's your father."

Dennis stopped.

Long enough for the man she so badly wanted to call her Boris to hobble into the truck and drive away.

Bree didn't look at him. She didn't want to see him go. And yet part of her was glad when he did. As much as she had yearned for him, spent so many years gilding his memory, this mortifying scene had tarnished her fantasy forever. The need to minister to her son, tend to his upset and shock, was far more important than any carnal desires she might have had for the swearing Mexican.

It was never the way she imagined telling Dennis.

In no way ideal.

He would have killed him otherwise.

That would have been a greater sin.

William allowed Madeline the right to disappear, although essentially it was a token one. Within a matter of weeks, her new abode could be seen on Google Earth and viewed from the comfort of any home computer.

Her lawyer had contacted him.

They'd come to a simple agreement.

He would stay in the house until the end of the academic year and then it would be put on the market and sold. William gave up any claims on a share of the sale, although it promised to be lucrative. Even allowing for the money she'd pumped into it, the house had appreciated enormously. He had to give her credit for proving so astute about the renovation.

He continued teaching, or rather, going through the motions of going to class and teaching. It was probably as well that he'd given notice. He would have been fired if he wasn't already leaving. Judging by the whispers and stares when he appeared in class, his students were scandalized by his demeanor and tardiness. William was surprised they were all so puritanical. In his day, students had been a bunch of vagabonds.

When he wasn't teaching, he was sleeping. That is, in between bouts of drinking.

Way to go.

Bunny was called in to do her shtick.

William was actually pleased to see her. Those sliding silicone cheeks. Those lips that looked as though they had been smooshed across her face. He heard her with a client in the bedroom, extolling the lavish refurbishment, the ample closet space and its celebrity provenance. A voice had drawled: "Was this where she died?"

He was grateful for Bunny's reply. "She's not dead, hon. She's doing an online degree."

He was glad she sounded so certain. That made perfect sense, Madeline studying, although he had to wonder where Bunny was getting her information—probably from the same place as he. The Internet, of course.

He was in the house looking out on the garden.

Bees humming in the lavender.

A cicada chirruped somewhere.

He saw sweetness in the golden poppies she'd planted.

Our state flower, she'd said without irony.

The life they might have had together.

A "landscape specialist" would tear them up and install some high maintenance water-unwise monstrous edifice. No profit in wildflowers.

The thought of it made him angry. Then a bewildering sadness.

He felt like weeping, but he couldn't. Tears would have been profligate, self-pity and *vino rosso* trying to fashion tragedy out of failure. To cry for a love that was all desire and mirrors, flashbulbs and Word documents would be revisionist. No rewrites would change what was done. He could read the consequences of his actions.

Dennis once asked him if he worked for Miss Brooks.

Not even that . . .

T he day before he was due to leave for New York, he drove out to the desert. He wanted to see her one last time.

She was living several miles northeast of Indian Wells, not far from the highway, a forlorn bypass inhabited by the migrant workers who serviced the lush oasis.

Down a dusty track.

Past scattered dwellings, barely more than shacks.

Tufts of scrub spotted like an old man's stubble.

No irrigation to pretend the land was anything other than it was: harsh and unforgiving, quietly teeming with life.

But the light was good and he couldn't argue with a big sky.

Her bungalow sat on a small parcel of land, with the whipped mocha crests of the San Bernardinos stretching both ways behind. The house was modest, prefabricated twenty years before. Lying at an angle to the natural topography of the foothills, it had the look of a Lego house dropped randomly in the burro brush by a careless child. At first he was surprised by her new home's lack of privacy: there was a small buffer of land to the fence, but not so much that you couldn't see inside her kitchen. Then he realized that she was fed up with hiding or wanted to be found. There was probably no difference.

A photographer was already standing outside her fence, a long-lensed camera dangling from his neck. He took a picture of William before propping himself up against her gate and settling into conversation. He introduced himself as Hal Brooks. "No relation," he'd said with a grin. "It's been a zoo here up until a few days ago. Now everyone's gone back to LA. Something's going down with T's boyfriend." William disliked his confidential tone and the presumption that he knew or cared about "T." He realized that there was a formula to how long the crowd stayed on the celebrity perimeter; a sliding scale, proportionate to the subject's length of time as a star. Madeline hadn't been a star that long.

According to Hal, Madeline had few visitors, only a couple of women he didn't recognize. She went out only to the supermarket and the taco stand and spent time tending plants in pots around the back. Occasionally she went farther afield to the national park.

Madeline had taken William to Joshua Tree before their wedding. As they'd only decided to marry the week before, there was no time to organize a dress or a party—even Romy wasn't available at such short notice. William and Madeline had both agreed that there was beauty and simplicity to a small, low-key, civil ceremony. While they waited for licenses to be procured, they'd stayed at a pretty hacienda-type hotel, which quickly became overrun with journalists and photographers who had to be cordoned off outside. Wherever William and Madeline went, they were surrounded by strangers, beaming felicitations at them. William felt slightly nauseous, as if out to sea on a cruise ship with no possibility of escape, having won the Grand Prize in the raffle. He realized that for all the right reasons he needed to try and get along with everyone, but he wasn't sure how he felt or whether any of it could be sustained. They'd sneaked out early, managing to avoid their followers by wearing clothing, Stetsons, and eye gear bought in the hotel gift shop. Madeline was proud to take him to a place of special significance; somewhere so outstanding where she'd camped with her father as a child. She was in awe of the vast primordial landscape, the giant rock formations unmoved and unchanged in centuries. She said it was the only place where she felt alive to the grand scale of time. Far from making her feel insignificant, a blip on the landscape, she said it made her feel more permanent, part of Earth's great and mysterious cycle. Only there did she feel fully attuned. She marveled at the desert blooms, the elegant occatillos, persimmon flowers waving at them from the tips of their branches, and said how deceptively cute the fuzzy cholla cacti looked. He'd seen it all through her eyes and for a moment he saw it again, the closest he'd been to equilibrium and joy. What people meant by happiness.

She passed by the window and looked out.

Her neck seemed to have cleared up and she seemed to have gained a little weight. She always said that chocolate gave her "zingers," which was why she avoided it. He wondered whether she had been eating chocolate—and why not?

He knew his speculations were laughable, worthy of a website. *That or shoot myself.*

Then she turned around and disappeared from sight.

He couldn't tell if he had been seen.

As he drove away, William was filled with admiration for her. In her trailer-trash incarnation, she was so much more interesting than when they'd been together playing the bourgeois couple. The courage and determination it must have taken to leave was impressive. He'd read about such people who upped and left in newspapers and novels. There was a book he'd particularly admired about a Belfast housewife who walks out on her husband and child to a circumstance more bleak than the one she'd left behind. Yet she was transcendent if only because the decision was authentically hers. William even had a stab at his own version—the janitor story—but he hadn't had the commitment to do justice to the cause. He couldn't find a way to make the purity of the act outweigh its inherent selfishness.

He would always stand by his reasons for showing her the tape.

He was glad when he was finally airborne. He felt better. So much more like his usual self.

He decided that as soon as he arrived in the city, he'd drop his bags at Ian's and then would go and look in on Esther. It had been twelve months since he'd been in touch with her. He'd stopped calling because she never answered the phone, and the rare occasion when Jujo could be enlisted to put her on, sitting on the end of a silent receiver was singularly unfulfilling.

There was still a possibility that she was alive.

He had a theory about Esther. How she'd managed to stay alive, one of nine hundred left in the ghetto, when almost a quarter of a million had died of disease or starvation or had been transported away for extermination. After failing to make her desperate bargain with the Gestapo officer, her mother was shot—not for her audacity but for the lack of sexual promise evidenced by an emaciated body. Esther had offered herself to the commandant, and thus ensured her survival. No surprise that she was never able to have a relationship or that she never married. Her obsession with William was some sort of transference. Men were saviors but they were also harbingers of death.

He was actually looking forward to seeing her.

There was always the chance she would tell him the end of her story.